The Perils of
Peppermints

The Perils of Peppermints

BARBARA BROOKS WALLACE

ATHENEUM BOOKS FOR YOUNG READERS
New York   London   Toronto   Sydney   Singapore

Atheneum Books for Young Readers
An imprint of Simon & Schuster Children's Publishing Division
1230 Avenue of the Americas
New York, New York 10020
Book design by O'Lanso Gabbidon
The text of this book is set in Bembo.
Printed in the United States of America
First Edition
10 9 8 7 6 5 4 3 2 1
Library of Congress Cataloging-in-Publication Data
Wallace, Barbara Brooks.
The perils of peppermints / by Barbara Brooks Wallace.
p.   cm.
Sequel to: Peppermints in the parlor.
Summary: Left at a New York boarding school by Aunt and Uncle Twice, eleven-year-old Emily finds horrors even greater than those she faced at Sugar Hill Hall, especially after she gets word that her inheritance is lost.
ISBN 0-689-85043-3
[1. Boarding schools—Fiction. 2. Schools—Fiction. 3. Swindlers and swindling—Fiction. 4. Inheritance and succession—Fiction. 5. Orphans—Fiction.] I. Title.
PZ7.W1547 Pd 2002
[Fic]—dc21   2001046361

*For the two royals of Clan Wallace,
Victoria and Elizabeth,
with love*

Contents

1

Terrifying Arrangements

The black cab rumbling through the city at nightfall swayed and shook with every gust of icy wind that blasted down the streets. Its roof was piled so dangerously high with bundles, boxes, and baggage that the cab further distressed its three occupants by very nearly tipping over each time it rounded a corner.

Inside the cab, no one spoke, each one being deep in thought. The only sounds heard were the drumming of the horses' hooves, the *chink-chinking* of their harnesses, and the clicking of sleet hurling itself against the windows.

Emily Luccock, one of the three inside the cab, sat rigidly by one window, clutching the seat in fright with each lurch and shudder of the cab. Why was she not the one seated in the middle between her Aunt and Uncle Twice, their arms around *her* comforting *her*? Did she not deserve that now when within the hour she was to be abandoned to who knew what fate? Had they chosen to dismiss from their minds all recollection that she was a young girl of still but eleven years, and that they were all the family she had left in the world? It seemed so to Emily, because it was Aunt Twice who sat in the middle of the seat, with Uncle Twice's arm about *her* shoulders, his arm tightening protectively each time the cab seemed in danger of turning over.

It tightened again when suddenly Aunt Twice began to tremble. "Oh, William," she moaned, "if it is this bad here, how will it be on the high seas? How will we be able to abide it?"

"My sweet girl," replied Uncle Twice, "I've been assured that we are sailing on the most modern of ships. Our cabin will offer every comfort. As for this weather, why, when we reach India it will be so warm you'll soon be longing to see a snow-flake!"

Uncle Twice's attempt at humor to cheer his "sweet girl" was clearly not very successful. She only sighed deeply and shook her head. Emily, for her part, could only think, *India . . . with the warm sun, the elephants, the tigers, and the temple bells. India, where they are going without me!*

Was it possible that at the very last moment, when the time for parting actually arrived, Aunt and Uncle Twice would have a change of heart, would relent and tell Emily she could go with them? She would cling to that hope until they reached the very docks, though it was a fast-fading hope. After all, had she not pleaded with them endlessly all the way on the train trip to New York? And what had that availed her? Nothing!

Why was all that Emily had already suffered not enough to persuade them that she should accompany them? Was it not enough that her mama and papa were no more, lost in a terrible boating accident? Orphaned once, was she to be made to feel orphaned again? And what of all the horror that had happened afterward? Was that not misery enough? Perhaps they did not see it all as clearly as she still did, each scene in her mind so terrible and real.

She saw herself, an orphan arriving at Sugar Hill Hall, the grand mansion in San Francisco that was home to Aunt and Uncle Twice, so named because Aunt Twice was sister to Emily's own

mama, and Uncle Twice brother to her papa. With
the loss of Mama and Papa, Emily was to live with
them.

Then there she was in that terrifying moment,
stepping through the doors of Sugar Hill Hall. In
the parlor were standing those who turned out to
be two of the most wicked, cruel, evil ladies ever
to be met in this world, Mrs. Meeching and Mrs.
Plumly.

The parlor itself had become shabby and deso-
late, for Sugar Hill Hall had been turned into
a home for sad old people abandoned by their
families, with Meeching and Plumly, Inc., the pro-
prietors. Aunt Twice herself had become shabby
and downtrodden as well. No longer the golden-
haired, sparkle-eyed beauty she once was, she was
now their servant. And there was no sign, not then,
not at any time, of handsome, dashing Uncle
Twice!

The scenes marched grimly on. There was Emily
in her tiny, dank cellar room where she was to live,
having now herself become a servant in Sugar Hill
Hall. There was the dismal dining room, where the
old people feasted on moldy bread and fish-head
stew and tea made from a single tea bag passed

around the table. There was the scene of Emily being tormented by Tilly, the other servant girl. And then came the chilling vision of herself imprisoned in the dreaded Remembrance Room in the cellar, the place where the old people were locked up for stealing a peppermint.

Oh, those murderous peppermints! Emily would never, never forget, no never, that table in the parlor with the red velvet cover decorated with gold tassels, on which rested that bowl of puffy, tempting, tantalizing, delicious pink-and-white-striped peppermint drops, placed there deliberately to entice some poor old person into reaching out a hand and taking one. More than anything else, Emily would never forget *that*!

But then, at long last, everything had miraculously come to rights. The confession of a dying sea captain had revealed that Uncle Twice, who through gambling and a wild life (later sorely regretted) had lost all his fortune save Sugar Hill Hall itself, was not guilty of the murder of which he was accused by Meeching and Plumly, Inc. It was they themselves who were guilty of the murder of a seaman, along with the captain himself. So Uncle Twice could return safely from exile working as a seaman aboard the ship *Silver Sea* and take his place as the rightful owner of Sugar Hill Hall. Meeching and Plumly, who proved to be smugglers as well as murderers, not to mention their making plans to do away with Emily and Aunt Twice, were taken off to jail in chains.

Oh, what joy and happiness then reigned in Sugar Hill Hall for Emily; Aunt Twice; the old people; Kipper, the fishmonger's son, who was Emily's true friend throughout; and even Tilly, who proved to be not nearly so wicked as Emily had supposed.

But, alas, the happiness lasted for only a few paltry weeks. Uncle Twice was soon to be seen wandering the grand rooms of Sugar Hill Hall, silent, sunk in somber thought, his brows often drawn together in a deep frown. Aunt Twice's face began once more to look pale and drawn. But nobody explained why, until one sad afternoon, when Emily was finally invited to sit down before both of them.

"Do you remember, Emily, when you first came to Sugar Hill Hall, and I said you must try to be a brave little girl?" Aunt Twice asked.

Emily nodded solemnly. How well she remembered those very words!

"Well," Aunt Twice continued, "once again, I must ask you the same thing."

"But—but why?" stammered Emily. "All is happiness now, isn't it?"

Uncle Twice shook his head sadly. "The happiness is that I have been able to return to my family a man no longer accused of any crime," he said. "But as for the rest, I'm afraid I must now pay for all those early years when I carelessly squandered my fortune until there was nothing left."

"Not nothing, Uncle Twice," said Emily. "You still have Sugar Hill Hall."

"No longer, Emily," said Aunt Twice with a sob. "Oh, tell her, William!"

"Sugar Hill Hall has been sold," said Uncle Twice, his face twisted with grief.

"S-S-Sold?" Emily felt as if her heart would stop. "Why?"

"To pay all my terrible debts, Emily," replied Uncle Twice, "waiting for me when I returned. With no money left to pay them, and none with which to run this mansion, I had no choice but to sell it."

"But what about the money left to me by Mama and Papa?" cried Emily. "Kipper once said

I was a 'hairess.' Doesn't that mean I have lots and lots of money? Can't you take that, Uncle Twice?"

Uncle Twice shook his head firmly. "Never, never would Aunt Twice and I touch that, dear Emily. *Never!* That money is a sacred trust to be used for your future needs. Nothing more is to be said about it. No, I have made my bed, and I must lie in it!"

"But where will we live?" Emily moaned. "What of the old people who were to stay here? What of Tilly?"

"Welcoming homes have been found for them all, as we shall now tell them," replied Uncle Twice. "There are no worries on that score."

"Well," said Emily with a firm bob of her head, trying to be a "brave little girl" as Aunt Twice had requested, "at least *we* shall all be together!"

But at this, Aunt and Uncle exchanged telling glances. Each seemed waiting for the other to speak. At last it was Aunt Twice who said hesitantly, "Not—not *all* of us, Emily darling, at least not for now."

Not *all* of them? Could it be that Uncle Twice must leave Aunt Twice and Emily again? No, not even just Emily, for the happy announcement had been made that there was to be a Baby Cousin Twice!

"Oh, Uncle Twice!" cried Emily. "Must you go away once more? How can you leave Aunt Twice *now*?"

Once again, Aunt and Uncle Twice exchanged glances. Aunt Twice's hands were clasped so tightly together, her knuckles had grown white. "Uncle Twice will not be leaving *me*, dear child," she said. "I will be going with him."

Emily's breath caught in her throat. "But—but what about *me*?" she gasped.

"William," said Aunt Twice, tears in her eyes, "you must explain what has happened to Emily so she will understand everything."

Explain what has happened? Understand everything? Understand *what*? It sounded frightening. And by the time Uncle Twice had made his explanations, Emily did indeed understand all . . . and it was more frightening than ever!

It appeared, said Uncle Twice, that though they were to receive a handsome sum from the sale of Sugar Hill Hall, there would not be enough left to pay all his debts and still provide a means for their livelihood, especially now with the forthcoming arrival of Emily's Baby Cousin Twice. But then a remarkable solution to their dilemma had come about through the lawyer who represented the purchaser of Sugar Hill Hall. Although the purchaser was from another city and was someone neither Aunt nor Uncle Twice had known or ever met, Uncle Twice had been taken with Mr. Slyde, the lawyer, and had struck up a friendship with him.

Learning of Uncle Twice's predicament, Mr. Slyde told him of a small British company the elderly owner of which had died, leaving heirs who had no interest in the business. Uncle Twice could buy it for the money provided by Sugar Hill Hall, and would thus own a business and have income as well to support his growing family. It meant Uncle Twice must go to India for an extended period of time, but it was too splendid an opportunity to be dismissed.

India! India, where it appeared that Aunt Twice could accompany Uncle Twice, but not Emily. British families in India sent every school-age child back to England, and Emily would have to be sent away as well. Oh, not to England, but to New York, where one day Aunt and Uncle Twice would return. So it was best for her to remain behind and be placed in a boarding school. And it turned out Mr. Slyde could be of help there as well, for he was acquainted with a very exclusive, elegant establishment, so exclusive and elegant, in truth, that one young girl who attended it was a member of a royal family! Emily had already been registered there, and so it was all settled that she was to be a student and boarder at the exclusive, elegant Mrs. Spilking's Select Academy for Young Ladies.

Emily cared not a whit how exclusive and elegant it was. She did not wish to be separated from Aunt and Uncle Twice. She did not wish to go there. But her arguments against it could not change anyone's mind. Even the one about money! For where, pray tell, would that come from to pay for this exclusive, elegant establishment? Well, in this worthy case, Uncle Twice would allow for her own fortune to be used, it seemed. He had seen to it that it was all safely invested, and Mr. Slyde entrusted with full authority to administer it while Uncle Twice was away in India.

When Emily argued that, after all, she had not been attending school when she was living in the cellar as a servant girl, she was only met with the reply that it was all the more reason she should miss no more. Her insistence that she could read lots of books in India and be as educated as she needed to be fell on deaf ears. In the end, these and every other argument she could think of were rejected. And Emily began to suspect why.

All concentration was to be on Baby Twice, and there would be no time left over to worry about Emily. This was only Emily's suspicion, of course, but more and more she was hearing "Emily darling" being replaced with "Baby darling" in Aunt and Uncle's conversations! Emily, once the only child in their lives, was to be the only child no more.

And even in the rattling black cab taking them to the docks, it was Aunt Twice who was of greatest concern to Uncle Twice. Further, though Emily knew the train, arriving when it did, made them believe they must go directly to the docks rather than first take Emily to her school, could they not have tried a little harder to arrange for that? Why must she now have to be met and transported to the school like a piece of baggage by a strange man, also arranged by the accommodating Mr. Slyde?

But it was clear that Aunt and Uncle Twice's thoughts were entirely on what lay ahead of them, and Emily, whose future they considered settled, was already as far from their minds as if they had already arrived in India.

The horses' hooves drummed on. Through the windows of the cab, Emily could see men with their collars turned up against the sleet and icy wind, and women clutching their coats around themselves, all fighting to get to their warm homes as quickly as possible. The rattling cab piled high with boxes and baggage meant nothing to any of them. And it certainly meant nothing to them that one of the three passengers within that cab was a young girl who sat there in silence, her heart breaking.

2

Ichabod Crawstone

They reached the docks at last. The cab, swaying precariously, came to a groaning stop before a bleak gray building strung across with windows so encrusted with grime that they served no purpose at all. Herded by Uncle Twice, along with Aunt Twice, Emily entered a dank, cavernous room of the building. Ugly gas lamps overhead glared down upon swarms of dockworkers wheeling carts loaded with crates, ships crewmen shouting orders, and prospective passengers, all looking frozen and miserable as they huddled around their portmanteaus and carpetbags, looking vainly for help in boarding the waiting ship. The ship could be seen through wide openings that fronted the dock. It appeared a dark, mysterious hulk that even rows of lighted portholes could not make inviting in the icy wind and sleet howling past it.

But as they cautiously made their way across the room toward a glass enclosure bearing a sign that read INFORMATION AND ASSISTANCE, Emily's attention was suddenly caught and held by one thing, the man standing in front of the enclosure. He was dressed entirely in black, a color that extended even to a heavy, clipped beard. Unlike others around him, he appeared indifferent to the cold. He was not hunched down into his coat, nor did he even have his rich fur collar pulled up about his neck. Tall and narrow, black leather-gloved hands motionless at his sides, he may well have been a steel post as he stared at the three of them threading their way across the room.

For no reason that she could explain, the sight of this man frightened Emily. Was he a ghastly portent of dreaded things to come? No! No! He was only a stranger who happened to be standing there. He had nothing to do with her, and she was letting her fears get the better of her. Yet before they had even quite reached the glass enclosure, to Emily's horror, the man stepped forward.

"Would you be Mr. and Mrs. Luccock?" he asked.

"Why, yes, indeed!" Uncle Twice replied quickly. "And you must then be—"

"Ichabod Crawstone, at your service," the man interrupted, bowing slightly.

"Mr. Crawstone, we do apologize for keeping you waiting even a moment. We were slightly held up in tending to our baggage, which had to be unloaded from our cab and dealt with by a porter. We wouldn't want to inconvenience you for the world. Mrs. Luccock and I are so grateful to you for taking care of our niece for us. We don't know what we would have done if . . ." Uncle Twice shook his head, his voice trailing off.

"Think nothing of it," said Mr. Crawstone. "And you must know there is little I would not do for Josiah Slyde. I am deeply indebted to him for past kindnesses, and when he asked of me this small favor for a friend, I was only too happy to oblige. This, I presume, is the young person to be put in my charge?"

"It is, indeed!" said Uncle Twice, putting his arm about Emily and propelling her toward Mr. Crawstone.

"How do you do, Emily," said Mr. Crawstone, smiling at her.

But it was a smile that made Emily feel an icy chill creep over her skin. It was a smile formed by the thinnest of lips drawn back over unnaturally tiny yellow teeth. It was a smile that traveled no further than the mouth, for the eyes behind narrowed lids were dark and hard, with no trace of any smile ever having been in them.

"H-H-How do you do," Emily barely whispered, and quickly dropped her own eyes.

Aunt Twice, who as they crossed the room had done little but cast fearful glances at the foreboding hulk that was to carry them across the storm-tossed ocean, now at last turned her full attention to Emily.

"Oh, Mr. Crawstone!" she cried. "This is not what we would have wished, to send our beloved niece to a school without even being able to see it ourselves."

"Madam, you need have no fear," replied Mr. Crawstone. "For although I have never visited the school myself, it comes with the highest of recommendations. And so I was pleased to be able to tell Josiah when he made inquiries on your behalf. You have my assurance, madam, that your niece will be provided with the best education in the most pleasant surroundings. And I also assure you she will be in a school with other young ladies whose families demand the absolute finest."

"I do hope all you say is true! Oh, I do hope so! If for a moment we were to think that . . ." Unable to go on, Aunt Twice wrung her hands, a sob caught in her throat.

But if she *had* gone on, what could she have said, anyway? That if things were not as Mr. Crawstone had described them, she and Uncle Twice would return to fetch Emily and whisk her off to India? Why not just take her now and be done with it?

Emily wanted to throw her arms around Aunt and Uncle Twice, begging them one last time to take her with them. Yet how *could* she under the cold, unsympathetic eyes of Mr. Crawstone? All she could do was stand and listen to Uncle Twice explaining to him that her trunk had been sent on to the school, and that the little portmanteau at her feet was all that needed to be of any concern. And then the terrible moment came when it was clear that time had run out, and all hope with it. With promises from Aunt and Uncle Twice of long and frequent letters, Emily's replies to which they would eagerly await, Aunt Twice tearfully hugged her. After one last hug from Uncle Twice, they were gone. Looking back once as she left the building with Mr. Crawstone, Emily could no longer see any sign of Uncle Twice's fair head or Aunt Twice's ruffled blue velvet bonnet bobbing along beside him. They had vanished entirely.

Whatever charm Mr. Crawstone had seen fit to draw from his small supply of that commodity in her aunt and uncle's presence, he clearly saw no reason to waste any more on Emily. He did not even offer to carry her portmanteau, as Uncle Twice had done. And he appeared entirely indifferent to the bumping and thumping of the portmanteau against her knees as she struggled to keep up with his long strides.

And while Emily might never have imagined a more miserable ride than the one she took to the docks with Aunt and Uncle Twice, the one to Mrs. Spilking's Select Academy for Young Ladies surely surpassed it. Mr. Crawstone seemed totally committed to sitting in stony silence, staring out the window. This left Emily no choice but to do the same.

How, she asked herself over and over again,

could Aunt and Uncle Twice have left her in the charge of such a person? Were they so blinded by their own affairs that they had failed to note Mr. Crawstone's thin-lipped smile that was not a smile and his cold eyes? Worse yet, had they indeed noticed, but were so afraid something might go amiss in disposing of Emily that they were willing to overlook the qualities of anyone who had come to fetch her, no matter how dreadful they were?

But who was there in that cab to answer these questions? As Emily sat with white, high-button shoes crossed and hands folded politely in her lap, the answers came only in the *clop-clopping* of the horses' hooves, the *click-clicking* of the never-ending sleet against the windows, and the lonely gaslights winking palely at her as the cab rolled by them.

On and on the cab rolled, with Emily losing all sense of how far they had gone, how many streets crossed, how many corners turned. All this without a word spoken. Some of the streets were crowded with cabs, wagons, and throngs of people, despite the lateness of the hour. But when the cab finally drew to a stop, it was on a street that was deserted.

Feeble gaslights barely lit up lonely skeletal trees, their ghostly reflections dancing eerily on darkened windows that gave no evidence of life behind them.

They had stopped before the most ordinary of narrow brick houses, with no distinguishing features whatsoever. Further, it was attached to a row of other ordinary narrow brick houses that stretched from one end of the block to the other. In truth, the whole street as far as the eye could see was made up of very nearly identical houses.

Emily's heart fell like a stone. Although she had not formed any firm opinion of what the school she would attend should look like, somehow she did have the idea that any school attended by a member of a royal family ought to be at least partly as grand as Sugar Hill Hall. That was the only thought that from time to time had helped lift her sagging spirits. So how could this plain narrow building on this dreary street be the right place? Could the cabdriver have misunderstood the directions? Surely Mr. Crawstone, to whom the school had been so highly recommended, would be as puzzled as Emily by this and would question the driver. But instead, he simply threw open the door and climbed down from the cab.

"This is it. Come along!" he said tersely. "You will wait here for me, please," he ordered the cabdriver. Then he swiftly climbed the brick steps to the plain painted brown door and raised the knocker.

If there was any remaining question in Emily's mind as to possibly being in the wrong place, it was instantly dispelled by the brass plaque hanging beside the door. Therefore, she knew when she stepped through the doorway that she had indeed for the first time stepped into Mrs. Spilking's Select Academy for Young Ladies.

But as for the owner of the academy, Emily never noticed that the woman who answered the door was not in a costume befitting the caretaker of a member of a royal family. Never noticed that she was in only a dull gray dress, with a narrow white band at the collar the only form of adornment—unless one was to consider the narrow belt from which dangled a large assortment of ominous keys on a dull brass ring. And never noticed that dark hair twisted into a stern bun pierced with a plain black comb atop her head did nothing to improve upon the pinched, sharp, bloodless face beneath it.

No, what Emily *did* notice was that the woman instantly lowered her face, pursing her lips in a way that suggested she had caught Emily in some wicked misdeed. With ice-green eyes flaring, she fixed Emily with an unblinking stare, seeming to be completely indifferent to the presence of Mr. Crawstone. In confusion, Emily quickly lowered her eyes. That was when she first saw the large black dog by the woman's side. Emily barely heard the door click shut behind her, because at the same moment, the dog growled, a deep, throaty, frightening growl.

Its collar was attached to a heavy iron chain, held with such white-knuckled intensity by the woman that it was evident if the dog were released, anyone in its way would be in grave peril. All of this—the pursed mouth, the flaring eyes, the tightly restrained dog—was certainly for Emily's benefit and clearly to serve as a warning. Oh, yes, a very clear warning, indeed!

But of what? And, oh, most particularly, why?

3

Mrs. Spilking's Select Academy

Any fleeting thought Emily had that this might be only a housekeeper and not Mrs. Spilking herself who had come to answer the door was quickly put to rest.

"I am Mrs. Spilking," she said. "And this is Emily Luccock, whom I have been told to expect, is it not?" She looked questioningly at Mr. Crawstone.

"It is, indeed," he replied with a small, stiff bow. "Allow me to present myself. I'm Ichabod Crawstone, commissioned by a friend of Miss Luccock's aunt and uncle to escort her here. And now that I've fulfilled my duty . . ." Mr. Crawstone put his hand on the door as if to leave.

"Oh, Mr. Crawstone," said Mrs. Spilking quickly. "You must permit me to invite you into my humble parlor to warm yourself by a small fire before going back out into this icy storm. Please do consider it."

Mr. Crawstone hesitated, then withdrew his hand from the door. "That's very kind, Mrs. Spilking. Why, yes, I do accept your kind offer."

"Splendid!" Mrs. Spilking pursed her lips again, but it was a purse that contained something far more inviting than was offered to Emily. "Come along, Emily. We will go into my parlor, where I will ring for the housemaid to escort you to your room. You may bring your portmanteau with you."

Keeping the dog tightly at her side with the chain, Mrs. Spilking proceeded down the narrow hallway, followed by Mr. Crawstone and Emily, *thump-thump-thumping* along with her portmanteau. The hall was only dimly lit by two fluttering gaslights set high in the wall, and furnished with but one stiff-backed wooden bench and a strip of carpet underfoot, Oriental to be sure, but thin, worn, and frayed at the edges.

But at the end of the hall, not too many feet from where stairs rose up to a dark landing, Mrs. Spilking led them into a room warmed by a fire crackling invitingly in the fireplace. On a hob in the fireplace, a teakettle hummed merrily. This room, her own private parlor it seemed, was cozy with plump, flowered chintz armchairs, lace doilies decorating tiny walnut tables, and at least a dozen bright, cheerful pictures of country scenes. On one of the tables reposed a fluted pink dish holding an array of miniature frosted cakes.

As soon as they entered the room, Mrs. Spilking quickly pressed a button, which produced the sound of a jangling bell somewhere in the far reaches of the building.

"Allow me to take your coat and hat, Mr. Crawstone," she said, as she carefully attached the dog's chain to a ring in the wall. "And won't you be seated? I hope you won't refuse a nice cup of hot tea?"

"I would be delighted, Mrs. Spilking," replied Mr. Crawstone, removing and handing her the garments requested.

"It's much too late to show Emily the school," said Mrs. Spilking. "That can all be taken care of tomorrow. You might be interested to know, Mr. Crawstone, that while the buildings appear narrow, we do have two of them."

"You have nothing to be ashamed of here, Mrs. Spilking," said Mr. Crawstone. "Your school came very highly recommended, as I was pleased to tell my friend, who sought my aid in behalf of Miss Luccock's aunt and uncle."

"Highly recommended!" exclaimed Mrs. Spilking. "That is flattering, indeed!"

Now, throughout all this exchange of pleasantries, Emily was left standing in her coat and bonnet, her portmanteau at her feet. She might well have been a girl standing in the middle of one of the paintings hanging on the wall for all the notice she was being given. And it was certain she was never to be invited to remove her coat and bonnet, to avail herself of a cozy chair, or to be offered a "nice cup of hot tea," much less one of the little frosted cakes.

But it was also certain that Mrs. Spilking was well aware of her presence, because at last she rose impatiently and rang the bell once more. "Now, where *is* that girl!"

The bell had no sooner finished jangling than "that girl" appeared, a lanky fifteen-or-so-year-old in a faded gray dress with part of the hem dragging and a disreputable white apron streaked with soot. Wisps of hair stuck out untidily from under a wrinkled mobcap that sagged around her sallow, thin face.

"Bella, this is Emily, a new student," said Mrs. Spilking. "I wish you to take her up to the room she is to occupy with Sarah and Lucy, as I am entertaining a guest at the moment. Where is your lantern? You know you must always be prepared with your lantern."

"I was, mum," said Bella without a flicker of an eyelash. "Saw lamps on in the hall, so left it in the dining room."

"Well, you may go then," snapped Mrs. Spilking. "Good night, Emily."

Emily was so startled at having her presence finally noted, she could barely mumble, "G-G-Good night, Mrs. Spilking. And—and thank you, Mr. Crawstone, for bringing me here."

Mr. Crawstone nodded his acknowledgment.

"And, Bella," said Mrs. Spilking as the two girls started from the room, "please do not appear in that condition again when you answer my bell."

"Yes, mum," replied Bella, rolling her eyes upward. She was careful, of course, to do this with only the back of her head visible to Mrs. Spilking.

Leaving Mrs. Spilking's room, Bella led Emily through a door across the hall where a plain long table with several straight-backed chairs around it were evidence that this was the dining room.

"Fancy a bisk?" Bella asked as she picked up a small lantern, already lit, sitting on a table against the wall.

"Bisk?" asked Emily, having never heard the word before.

Bella snickered. "Bisk-it, o' course. I figger you ain't had anything to eat. No chance in this world Mrs. Spilking would o' offered one o' them fancy little treasures she buys for herself and her royal majestry." Bella produced another telling roll of her eyes upward. "Anyways, offer still stands. You want a bisk?"

Emily had actually had nothing to eat since the noon meal aboard the train, and then only a hard roll and bit of cheese. Even a dried "bisk" sounded good at this point. She quickly nodded.

"Well, then," said Bella, "you wait whilst I go fetch it. I'll just snitch a couple o' bisks from the bisk basket and hope Madam S. don't go counting. Everything 'round here got a flippin' number on it."

Emily's breath caught in her throat. "Everything 'round here got a number on it." Wasn't that what Tilly had said on that first terrible night when Emily had arrived at Sugar Hill Hall?

"What—what would happen if you got caught?" she asked, trying to keep her voice from shaking.

Bella shrugged. "Oh, I might get sent back to Pa for a day. He'd wallop me 'round for a bit, then shoot me back here. He ain't having me home no more than Mrs. Spilking has intentions o' losing cheap help like me. But don't you worry. I'm good at not getting caught. Had lots of experience at it. You go park yourself on that bench out there. I'll be right back."

The bench was the one in the hallway. It was set against the wall between the door to Mrs. Spilking's parlor and the staircase. As soon as Bella had disappeared, Emily wished that she had asked to wait in the dark dining room instead of where she was. The door to Mrs. Spilking's room was not tightly closed, and a sliver of light streamed into the hallway. Further, Emily could hear the voices of Mrs. Spilking and Mr. Crawstone quite clearly. What if Mrs. Spilking were to come from her room and find Emily sitting there, for all intents and purposes eavesdropping? But Bella had told her to "park herself," and so, not certain if she should move, Emily remained "parked" on the bench. And though trying not to listen to the conversation coming from Mrs. Spilking's room, she was, despite herself, listening.

"Splendid cup of tea, Sophronia," said Mr. Crawstone.

"Thank you, Ichabod," replied Mrs. Spilking. Then she added coyly, "You may have noted a little drop of something added to keep you warm on your journey home."

"I have indeed noted it, Sophronia," said Mr. Crawstone, stealing a little more from his well-guarded supply of charm.

Sophronia? Ichabod? What was this all about, Emily wondered, rigid on her hard bench in the hall. How could Mrs. Spilking and Mr. Crawstone arrive in such a short time at the point where they were addressing each other familiarly by their first names? Even cold and unfeeling as he appeared to be, had Mr. Crawstone not questioned how a school so "highly recommended" could be so shabby and run by such a person as Mrs. Spilking? How could he now be sitting with her enjoying a cup of tea with "a little something in it"?

"I must say, Ichabod, it's a relief not to have had to put on the usual charade of showing the . . . um . . . *room* and all the rest," said Mrs. Spilking. "This is a great deal more pleasant."

"It is, Sophronia!" replied Mr. Crawstone. "It is!"

"Well, you certainly put on a convincing act in front of our little friend," said Mrs. Spilking. "You should go on the stage, Ichabod."

"I *thought* I did rather well," he replied. "Still, in the end, I suppose it doesn't matter much since, as you say, she'll never have the chance to tell all, even assuming she comes to know all."

"I'll take care of *that*, you may be sure," said Mrs. Spilking. "You *are* quite certain they are safely aboard the ship?"

"I saw them on their way with my own eyes," replied Mr. Crawstone. "I don't doubt at all that they are minutes away from being on the high seas."

"Splendid! Splendid!" said Mrs. Spilking.

What more they had to say Emily was not to know, because at that moment Bella tiptoed up and beckoned her toward the stairs. But as she followed Bella up, Emily's feelings were a mixture of rage and horror and pure terror. Had not Mr. Crawstone told Aunt and Uncle Twice that he had never visited this school? A lie! And everything that happened thereafter apparently a lie. Sophronia and Ichabod, indeed! They had known each other all along!

Yet what was the point of the lies? What difference could it make whether or not it was known that Mr. Crawstone was already acquainted with Mrs. Spilking? But most ominously, why would Emily never have the chance "to tell all," presumably to Aunt and Uncle Twice, who were now "safely aboard the ship"? And more ominously still, what was the "all" that Emily was not to tell?

Oh, why had Aunt and Uncle Twice so trusted Mr. Slyde that they had also put their trust in Mr. Slyde's friend Mr. Crawstone? Should they not have investigated the school more closely? Something sinister and terrible was happening to Emily, and she was powerless to stop it. Or was she?

Was not Mr. Crawstone's cab waiting for him in front of the school? Why not jump in and order the cabman to take her back to the docks? Yes, and then find the ship steaming away? Also, pay the cab with what? Aunt Twice had sewn into her trunk lining the two gold coins Uncle Twice had given her, and her portmanteau held nothing but a few of her necessary garments.

As soon as she could, she would write Aunt and Uncle Twice and tell them of the terrible mistake they had made. What they could then do about it she had no idea, but surely they would think of something. They would not possibly wish her to remain in such a place as this.

In the meantime, however, she was a prisoner of Mrs. Spilking's Select Academy for Young Ladies. There was no other way to put it. But the question was again . . . the question was *still* . . . why?

4

Sad Revelations

"Her flippin' majestry's room's that one," announced Bella when they reached the top of the stairs. She jerked a thumb over her shoulder toward a closed door at the front of the building. "Next door's the washroom, which she gets first go at when she wants it. No standing in line for *her*. If the other washroom's in use, everyone else just got to hold their breaths till she's through here. Hmmmph!" she snorted. "Only one gets to keep her door shut, too."

Bella now jerked the same thumb at the next door, which was, in truth, several inches ajar. Room sleeps two," she said. "Them are older girls been here longer than they ought, if anyone cares to know my opinion."

Emily actually cared very much to know Bella's

opinion about a great many things, but this was hardly the time to be asking—or even to be sharing confidences with someone she knew so little. At any rate, after struggling up the stairs with her portmanteau, she now had to give all her attention to simply keeping up with Bella.

Bella's thumb went back to work again as they turned at the head of the stairs and went through a doorway that must have been cut to join the two narrow buildings that made up the school. A second set of stairs just beyond the wall confirmed that. "Not for use excepting for me doing donkey work carrying laundry and the like," said Bella. "Madam S. wishes to know every girl what has to use stairs, so no sneaking up and down here. Now," again Bella's thumb was impressed into service, "there's the same room up front what's like her majestry's, only sleeps five. And here's the washroom for the rest. You take the lantern and go have a wash. I'll wait."

Grateful for the opportunity, Emily quickly availed herself of a room that did not invite anyone to remain there any longer than was absolutely necessary, with its bleak gray walls, cold linoleum, and worn granite basin with no mirror over it.

This without doubt insured the minimum of overflow into the room particularly reserved for royalty. Needless to say, Emily's washroom visit was speedily accomplished.

"This here's yours," said Bella, leading Emily through the door next to the washroom.

She found herself in a small room barely large enough to hold its one small pine chest of drawers and three brown-painted iron cots with a spindly pine chair next to each. Over the chest of drawers hung a little oval mirror so age spotted and clouded, the lantern flame hardly reflected in it at all. On the wall across from each cot was a coat hook, on two of which hung identical gray dresses. These clearly belonged to the occupants of the cots, two young girls at present fast asleep. The third cot, one under the window on the back wall, was empty.

Finger to her lips, Bella led Emily to the empty cot. "This is as far as you go. You got night stuff in that satchel?"

Emily nodded, setting her portmanteau on the piece of rag rug by the cot.

"Hey, what's this?" Bella lifted something from the foot of the cot. "Hmmmph! Looks like

Madam S. ain't wasting any time. It's your hew-nee-form waiting right here for you. Just hope it fits! I'll hang it up for you, then I'm out o' here. Don't want to be here when Madam makes her flippin' doggy run. Think you can finish up without the lantern?"

"Yes, I think so. B–B–But what's a doggy run?" Emily's voice quavered.

"Oh, it's just her cute little trick o' coming 'round with that dog o' hers, checking up on everyone." Bella shook her head with disgust. "Oops, almost forgot your bisks!" She dipped into her pocket and then thrust three hard little biscuits into Emily's hand. "Here you go. Just be careful 'bout crumbs. Eating in your room ain't 'lowed. You might o' guessed."

"Th–Th–Thank you, Bella. It's . . . it's—" Emily faltered, overcome by this small act of kindness.

"Aw, it ain't anything," Bella interrupted. "No need to go on about it. You take care o' yourself. Ain't anyone else going to!" And with that warning, Bella was gone.

Gone with her, of course, was the friendly lantern light. Darkness closed in around Emily. Nightdress on, clothes piled on the chair beside her, she climbed cautiously into her cot. The hair mattress was so thin she could feel the sharp springs under it, and her pillow was a hard lump under her head as she lay on her back staring up at the ceiling. Waiting!

Sure enough, it was not too long before she heard footsteps treading softly up the hall, with the occasional *click* of a dog's nails on the floor. As the footsteps came closer, Emily rolled on her side and snapped her eyes shut. In moments, she felt the heat of a lantern being held over her face and the sound of a dog panting beside her. One. Two. Three. Four. The seconds ticked by. It was unbearable. Finally, she felt the lantern heat leave her face, and then heard footsteps, accompanied by clicking nails, stealthily leave the room.

But even with this terror safely out of the way, Emily could not drop off to sleep. She felt as much alone as she had been when she had first arrived at Sugar Hill Hall and had been consigned to that grim little room in the cellar inhabited by only herself and rats. But at least there she always had Aunt Twice, as much a prisoner as Emily was, to be sure, but at least she was there. Now her aunt was on a ship already bound for far-off India, so that

Emily could not possibly "tell all," that mysterious, ominous "all"! Oh, why had Aunt and Uncle Twice abandoned her? Why had they left her here with no one to turn to?

Emily could hold back the tears no longer. But she did not want to waken the two strange girls in her room or let them know of her misery, so she turned over and buried her face in her hard little pillow to stifle her sobs. As a result, she never heard the squeak of bedsprings, the sound of a match being struck, or the bare feet padding softly across the floor.

It was not until she felt a hand on her shoulder and turned to see the tiny flutter of lantern flame turned low that she knew anyone was standing by her bed. Mrs. Spilking! It must be Mrs. Spilking returned to her room! With a start, Emily turned over, her heart in her throat. But she found herself looking not into the deadly face of Mrs. Spilking, but into the frightened faces of two young girls. The one holding the lantern glanced nervously over her shoulder at the doorway.

"We're not supposed to be up," she whispered. "I mean, unless we have to use the washroom. Mrs. Spilking says Wolf—that's her dog—will rip us to shreds if we're caught. Anyway, my name is Sarah." The weak flame in the lantern lit up a pair of remarkably clear blue eyes, but they were set in a pasty, narrow face with a pinched nose so red rimmed it must have been subject to frequent applications of a wiping rag. Her hair, a nondescript brown, dangled thinly around her shoulders.

"I'm Lucy," said the second girl, whose face, while equally pasty, featured a pug nose peppered with freckles and cheeks puffed out like pale apples. This was all topped with an untidy mop of red ringlets.

"We decided we were going to let the new girl, which is you, know in case she cried that it was all right," said Sarah.

"*We* cried when we came," said Lucy. "You're Emily, aren't you, the new girl?"

Emily nodded, quickly sitting up in her cot.

"Who—who is it who didn't want *you*?" Lucy asked timidly.

"I—I don't understand," stammered Emily.

"Well," said Sarah, pausing to wipe her nose on the sleeve of her nightdress, "we're both here because of stepmamas who don't want us around. Mine is really pretty, and she doesn't want anyone thinking someone as plain as me belongs to her. That's not what she says, though. She just made Papa believe I ought to be in boarding school. It was easy. She's so pretty, and now with the baby coming, she has Papa twisted 'round her little finger. I guess it's the way papas are. So here I am!"

"*I'm* here because my stepmama is not just pretty, but is lots, lots younger than my real mama was," Lucy said. "She doesn't like having anyone thinking she's the mama of someone who's as old as eleven. She thinks it makes *her* seem old. I'm not even certain she wants the baby that's coming in case it makes her look old as well, though she can't very well send the baby to boarding school. But Sarah's right. The real reason is never what they say. *Everyone* is here because someone doesn't want them, we think."

"Even—even the person of—of royal blood?" asked Emily.

"That's Princess Delilla," replied Lucy. "At least that's what we're expected to call her. But we don't know why *she's* here. We don't know anybody who does. It's a big mystery."

"But lucky for Mrs. Spilking she *is* here," said Sarah. "It makes the school sound grand to tell people someone royal is here. I expect your family was told that, weren't they?"

Emily nodded. That's exactly what they were told!

"Yes," Lucy chimed in, "and Mrs. Spilking gets to show off the princess's big pretty room to the families. But the other girls actually get put in rooms like this one. Mrs. Spilking is so afraid someone in Princess Delilla's country will take her back, we expect, she gets all the special treats. Sarah and I think she's spoiled as she can be, don't we, Sarah?"

Sarah nodded, scowling. "Yes, we do." Then she added wistfully, "We sometimes wish *we* were the princesses here. Then it might not be so bad."

"The way it is . . . ," Lucy began, first looking at Sarah, then fearfully back again at the doorway, "we—we *hate* it here!"

"Your families might take you back. Can't you write a letter to them about it?" asked Emily. After all, that was what *she* intended to do.

Lucy shook her head. "Mrs. Spilking reads all our letters, even those of the older girls, and mails them herself. Every morning we have penman-ship, and that's when once a week we write letters.

She checks every one before it gets sent. It's for spelling and grammar, she *says,* even though we write the same things every time."

"We ask how everyone is at home," Sarah broke in. "Then we tell them how happy we are and how much we're learning. Well, it's what they want to hear, anyway, and it's what Mrs. Spilking expects."

"And if anyone comes to call on us, we have to sit in Mrs. Spilking's parlor with Mrs. Spilking right there," said Lucy. "So how would we dare complain about anything?"

"Papa came to visit me at the beginning . . . once," Sarah said. "I had to tell him how glad I was to be here. I write that as well, and Papa always writes back how happy he is to hear it. I mean, when he remembers to write."

"It's exactly the same with me," Lucy said, and then hesitated. "But you never have said who it is who doesn't want *you.*"

"It—it isn't anyone," said Emily. "At least, I don't have a stepmama. My mama and papa are both no more, but my aunt and uncle who look after me had to go to India. All English children in India my age get sent back to England to go to school."

"Do American children get sent back to America as well?" asked Lucy.

"I—I guess so," replied Emily. "It's what they said, anyway. So they just left me here."

Sarah considered this a moment. "Well," she said, "it does seem as if you didn't get put here because you weren't wanted. I mean, unless your aunt's to have a baby and you'd be too much trouble to take along. She's not, is she?"

Slowly, Emily nodded.

"Oh!" said Lucy and Sarah, looking at her with sympathetic, pitying eyes.

Well, was that not what deep, deep down Emily had been thinking all along? No wonder the great Mr. Slyde had recommended Mrs. Spilking's Select Academy for Young Ladies. Everyone there was not wanted . . . a perfect choice for Emily!

"How—how long does everyone have to stay here?" Emily asked, remembering what Bella had said about the older girls.

Sarah shrugged. "We don't know, but we guess it's until our families marry us off to some old man wanting a young wife. Or perhaps we'll have to go off to be a governess or something like that."

"Well, that's never going to happen to me!"

cried Lucy, a sob in her throat. "I'll run away first. I haven't seen my grandpapa since my mama died. He's been at sea all this time. But perhaps if I can find him, he'd think of something."

"Lucy, you mustn't talk about running away," breathed Sarah, shuddering. "You know what Mrs. Spilking says. If we ever so much as set foot outside the school without her, she'll set Wolf on us. He can find us wherever we are, she says, and will tear us to shreds. But now we'd better get back to bed. What if they were to come again?"

Lucy's eyes flew open with fright at the thought of this possibility. "We'll see you in the morning, Emily," she whispered. And with one last trembling smile, the two girls ran swiftly back to their cots.

Once again in the darkness, foreboding thoughts began again to crowd into Emily's head. There was little question now as to why she was in Mrs. Spilking's Select Academy for Young Ladies. Not wanted! Every girl in that school was not wanted! Still, Aunt and Uncle Twice would surely write to her from India, and she would write back. Remembering Aunt Twice's tearful eyes at the boat dock, and Uncle Twice's warm hug, she could hardly believe they no longer cared for her, even if at the moment she was not wanted in their lives. Still, what exactly could she tell them?

All letters read by Mrs. Spilking! Is that not what Sarah and Lucy had said? Now Emily knew the meaning of Mr. Crawstone and Mrs. Spilking's assurances to each other that she would never be able to "tell all." Oh, how that ominous "all" kept returning to her thoughts! And though she could not explain why, except perhaps for "Sophronia" and "Ichabod" lying about knowing each other, she had the terrible feeling that the "all" applied only to her, and not to Sarah or Lucy or any other girl at the school.

Yet was there not something else that applied to her as well? The sudden thought made her heart beat faster. Was she still not an heiress? For the time being, Mr. Slyde was to manage her fortune, but she would come into it at seventeen. Marry an old man or become a governess, indeed! No, all she had to do was stick it out. Five years plus some months seemed an impossibly long time, but other girls had made it here that long, and she would do it. Yes, she would do it!

Her spirits considerably repaired, Emily now remembered all at once the "bisks" so kindly provided her by Bella. She wished now she had offered to share them with Sarah and Lucy, although they might well have been too frightened to accept them. So Emily pulled them out from the pocket of her coat lying on her chair, where she had hidden them, and lay nibbling on them in the dark. And thinking.

And when her eyes finally closed for sleep, her cheeks were dry. She had cried her first night at Sugar Hill Hall, and not again. Now she had finished with crying here. For she was remembering how she had survived the early horrors of Sugar Hill Hall: a wicked servant girl who only later proved to have a heart of gold as Bella did, a dank little cellar room, peopled only by rats, down the hall from the grim Remembrance Room, as opposed now to being in an upstairs room with two friendly young girls, and nothing more threatening down the hall than a spoiled princess. So if she could survive her introduction to Sugar Hill Hall, she could certainly survive all the charms provided by Mrs. Spilking's Select Academy for Young Ladies, including a vicious dog who might "tear her to shreds"! Yes, she could do it. She *would* do it! But, oh, if only there were not that short, terrible word hanging over her head.

"All"!

5

Oh No!

The loud, piercing sound of a jangling bell woke Emily rudely in the morning. Her mind still clouded from sleep that had been so long and late in coming the night before, she raised herself up to see that it was barely light outside her window. The window framed a frozen picture of ice-clad rooftops, a tiny, barren backyard, and beyond that an unkempt, empty lot. Emily shuddered at the sight of this cheerless landscape. She quickly turned from it to see that Sarah and Lucy had already made up their cots and were scrambling into their gray dresses.

"Hurry, Emily, hurry! We mustn't be late!" Even the dress being pulled over Sarah's head could not disguise the fear in her voice.

"It's three demerits if you're late to breakfast!"

Lucy breathlessly added her own dire warning. "It's on Mrs. Spilking's rule list right here on the door. You'll have to study it later. She expects us to know the rules by heart, every last one!"

Emily lost no time in dropping her feet to the floor and throwing her coverlet up over her cot. Climbing out of her nightdress and into her petticoat, she scurried to retrieve her own gray dress hung up by Bella. Bella's hopes that it would fit were in vain. The dress was way too large, and it was only by lifting the skirt and knotting the belt tightly around her waist that Emily was able to keep it from dragging on the floor. Then after pulling on her stockings and fastening her highbutton shoes with trembling fingers, she hurried from the room with Sarah and Lucy.

But it was only to have to stand at the end of a line, breathless, waiting to enter the washroom. The closed door signaled that the room was already in use, with four other girls queued up behind it. Through the doorway to the adjoining building, Emily could see two girls, older ones, who undoubtedly were the two referred to by Bella as having been there "longer than they ought." It seemed they were taking their chances on "her majestry" finishing before the other washroom became available.

Each girl, when she emerged from the washroom, went flying down the stairs. But when Emily had finished with her "turn," she was happy to see that Sarah and Lucy were waiting for her, though clearly frightened at doing so. Others were now standing there as well, the two older girls who had given up waiting for Princess Delilla to emerge from her washroom. That door was still tightly shut.

Her heart thumping, Emily followed Sarah and Lucy back to the hall she had entered the night before, and was led through the door behind the stairs into the dining room. The five other girls were already seated in straight-backed chairs at the one long table in the room. They sat in absolute silence, their hands folded on the table before them. At the head of the table sat Mrs. Spilking. From the time Sarah, Lucy, and Emily entered the room and took chairs across from the five girls, she stared at them with her eyes flaring and lips compressed. It was as if they were all being accused of something. Of what? Being late? How could they possibly have been down any sooner? The two oldest girls arrived moments later, one to take the chair next to Mrs. Spilking, the other the one next to the empty chair at the other end of the table.

The only other person in the room was Bella. She stood leaning on the wall beside the kitchen door, indifferently puffing on her fingernails and polishing them on her apron. Beside her was a serving cart, on which now lay only a large tin ladle.

As Emily could see, however, there was to be something more arriving, because in front of each girl was an empty china bowl, five matching and the rest plainly unmatched replacements. Beside each bowl was a spoon, and *none* of these matched. A white enamel pitcher was set in front of Mrs. Spilking, as well as a small, worn china bowl with only the memory of any painted design still remaining. This bowl contained . . . was it actually sugar? Emily was astonished. She had no idea what was finally to go into the bowls, but so far this was more promising than the fish-head stew and moldy bread lumps served the old people at Sugar Hill Hall. Yes, perhaps she really could stick it out at Mrs. Spilking's Select Academy for Young Ladies!

But so far, nothing was being served for them to eat. The girls continued to sit in silence, hands folded on the table before them, hands now including Emily's. The silence continued, until at last footsteps were heard on the stairs.

"Bella, you may now serve!" ordered Mrs. Spilking.

Bella immediately came to life and grabbed the handle of the serving cart as she prepared to race back with it to the kitchen. But before she could even get started, the kitchen door flew open. Out stumped an enormous woman in a faded pink dress, split at almost every visible seam. A mobcap drooping way to one side of her head and a sagging apron both made no pretense of ever having been anything but filthy and grease stained. Her face, round as a pot lid, and at the moment an angry red, was the setting for a pair of squinted eyes and several quivering chins. She was carrying a great, black iron pot, which she proceeded to slam down on the serving cart.

"I ain't got all day to stand la-da-da-ing in the kitchen stirring a blinkin' pot, waiting for her majestry to show up in the dining room!" she announced furiously. "I got a other job to go to and better things to do there. I should go and let this stuff burn on the stove. One day I will. Mark my words!"

"I am sorry for the inconvenience, Mrs. Slump," said Mrs. Spilking coldly. "But that will be quite enough."

"Not *nearly* enough!" growled Mrs. Slump, as she went thumping back through the door, giving it an extra shove to leave it swinging savagely behind her.

Mrs. Slump had no sooner disappeared, although the door was still trembling on its hinges, than "her majestry" the Princess Delilla came strolling in as if she had nothing whatsoever to do with the cause of the eruption.

If Emily had ever given any thought to what a princess should look like, she might very well have pictured her as this girl, except, of course, for her gray dress matching those of the others. Probably no more than fifteen years of age, she was tall and slender. Overshadowing an imperial nose and a perfectly formed mouth and chin were startlingly brilliant eyes, so green and slanted as to be almost catlike. A black ribbon tied back her glossy dark hair to reveal shapely ears wearing something probably not allowed any other girl there, earrings! They were only tiny gold balls, but earrings nonetheless. And finally, her cheeks could only be described as interestingly pale, not pasty as in the case of the other girls. All in all, it could not be denied that this princess was most decidedly . . . pretty!

But she was also decidedly pampered and, just as Lucy and Sarah had said, spoiled. Well, here she was never even opening her mouth to say she was sorry for being late. And Mrs. Spilking said not a word to her about it as she sauntered over and dropped into the chair at the head of the table. This was despite the fact that she had kept ten girls waiting for their meal, not to mention Mrs. Spilking herself, and created a major uproar on the part of Mrs. Slump.

As she was settling herself at the table and adjusting her skirt, however, Bella was already wheeling her cart to the head of the table, and had begun ladling gray, gluey lumps of porridge from the iron pot into the bowls, starting with Mrs. Spilking's. Emily was further astonished that Mrs. Spilking was to share the same unappetizing fare as that given the girls. This was a far cry from Sugar

Hill Hall, where Madams Meeching and Plumly ate nothing at all with the old people and then dined in high style in a private dining room later. But Emily finally decided that Mrs. Spilking eating with the girls was nothing but a sham, for Bella put such a small portion of the porridge in her bowl it was all but invisible.

Nonetheless, she continued the pretense by pouring milk from the enamel pitcher into her bowl. Or at least Emily supposed the substance pouring from the pitcher to be milk, though it was so thin and watered down as to be almost blue. Then, as this traveled down the table, Mrs. Spilking lifted the sugar bowl, and with a spoon no larger than a salt spoon, carefully sprinkled one spoonful into her bowl. Under her watchful, piercing glare, each of the five girls opposite Emily did the same.

But when the bowl reached the princess, she simply dumped a heaping spoonful into her bowl. Then a second. Then a third. She had helped herself to at least seven spoonfuls before passing on the bowl. But if Emily had any ideas of imitating this act, they soon evaporated when the older girl next to the princess, like all the other girls, carefully sprinkled one tiny spoon of sugar into her bowl.

Sadly, the few grains of sugar in connection with a thin, nearly blue liquid not much improved over plain water, did little to enhance a large, steaming lump of gluey, tasteless, gray porridge. Probably because they had finally become used to it, or simply because they were hungry and knew they could expect nothing better, the older girls seemed able to get most of it down. But Emily could choke down only a few bites, and she could see that Sarah and Lucy did not do much better. If only she had some of Kipper's pa's fish syrup that had done so much to increase the appetites of the old people of Sugar Hill Hall! But at last all spoons were laid down, and the dismal meal was ended.

"Bella, you may now clear," said Mrs. Spilking. "Adelaide, you will please fetch the stationery and pens for letter writing. Eudora, you will fetch the pots of ink."

So as Bella rushed the cart around the table collecting the bowls, spoons, milk pitcher, and sugar pot, two of the girls hurried to the sideboard. They returned to the table with the articles ordered by Mrs. Spilking, and passed them out to the girls still seated.

"Now," said Mrs. Spilking, "you will note that

our new girl, Emily Luccock, is with us, so I must explain what we are about to do, which is write letters. Time is allowed for this every week because I know all the girls' families long to hear from them, as I'm sure Emily's own family does." Mrs. Spilking paused to flare her eyes in Emily's direction. "You may begin now, girls."

Mrs. Spilking had, of course, said not a word about the fact that she would be reviewing the letters for spelling, grammar, or anything else. Nor had she even mentioned that the letters would pass through her hands for mailing. The other girls must know this, as did Sarah and Lucy. So the omission could only have been to let Emily hang herself from the very outset by writing her exact opinions of the school thus far. But thanks to Sarah and Lucy, Emily was quite prepared for it. So this is the letter she finally wrote:

Dear Aunt and Uncle Twice,

How was your exciting voyage to India? I hope it was fun and that you are both well.

I am so glad you learned about Mrs. Spilking's Academy from Mr. Slyde. I have only just come, but I believe I am going to like it a great deal.

I have a nice room that I share with two other girls, and we all wear neat gray uniforms.

My first breakfast has been a delicious porridge with milk and sugar, but I could not even finish mine, because we were all given such grand portions.

I expect to enjoy my lessons very much.

Hoping to hear from you soon, I remain your loving niece,

Emily

While Emily was writing, she once looked up to see Mrs. Spilking watching her with an eager gleam in her eyes and a half smile on her face. *Oh, yes,* said the look, *she is pouring her heart out to her aunt and uncle with every complaint she can think of. Well, we shall see about* that, *Miss Emily Luccock!*

When Emily had drawn her letter to an end and laid down her pen, she dropped her eyes guiltily, as if she had actually written the dreadful report expected by Mrs. Spilking.

"Well, I see we are all now finished, so just as we always do, we will now pass our letters in to me for spelling and grammar approval," said Mrs. Spilking, all the while never for a moment taking her eyes off Emily. "Now," she said as soon as all letters had been passed to her, "I shall first look at our new student's letter to see if she measures up to our academy standards."

From the way Mrs. Spilking's mouth twitched as she read Emily's letter, it would be safe to say that she was receiving a shock of a very unexpected and unpleasant nature. In the place of the frown and stinging rebuke she was prepared to deliver, she had instead to apply a forced smile to her face and tell Emily that she had, indeed, written a very nice letter. Further, as the spelling and grammar were flawless, she did not even have the pleasure of remarking on that. All that remained to be said was that she would see the letter was mailed at once to Emily's aunt and uncle in India.

Her plans in total disarray, Mrs. Spilking rushed through the other letters and then announced they would adjourn to the next room for their other studies and activities. Emily had begun to think the dining room was to be their sole classroom, but as the girls now rose from the table, Mrs. Spilking opened the wide pocket doors that led to a larger room at the front of the house.

Straight-backed chairs, each with a thin pillow on the seat, circled the room. In front of the chairs were long, low tables. On the table, before each chair, was a large cardboard box. At the head of the room, facing all the other chairs, was a faded purple, worn velveteen, high-backed wing chair. In front of the chair was also a table holding a large box. And to the side of that chair and table was . . . was . . .

Oh no! No! No! No!

Emily felt as if something had struck her hard in the chest. She struggled to take a breath as her legs began to buckle and finally give way entirely. Then blackness rolled over her, and she fell to the floor, senseless.

6

No Explanation

Emily had only the vaguest recollection of being helped up the stairs by two of the older girls. She could not remember being helped into her cot, however, or having someone undo and pull off her high-button shoes. But those things must have happened, because when she finally returned to her senses, she was indeed lying in her cot with her shoes off. But before then, she had been drifting in and out of a dark fog, not aware of anything. Later, she thought she remembered opening her eyes for a moment and seeing Mrs. Spilking peering down at her with narrowed, calculating eyes. Then the dark fog had rolled over her again.

When at last the fog lifted and did not return, Emily finally opened her eyes to see two scared faces looking at her, the faces of Sarah and Lucy.

"Oh!" cried Sarah, "you are all right, Emily. You had us so frightened."

"What happened to you?" asked Lucy. "Was it the dreadful porridge? Did it make you ill?"

"You—you'll get used to it," said Sarah uncertainly. "You just have to, Emily."

"I'll try. I really will," said Emily. "But—but it wasn't the porridge."

"What, then?" asked Lucy. "It could not have been because you were afraid of what you wrote in your letter. Mrs. Spilking said it was a nice letter. You were clever to write one like that, Emily."

"I remembered what you told me," said Emily. "But it wasn't that, either. It was—it was . . . the peppermints!"

The peppermints! Yes, *peppermints*! Peppermints in that very building! Peppermints in the room under the very floor where Emily lay in her cot! *They* were what had robbed Emily of all her breath, what had turned her legs to rubber, and finally sent the dark cloud rolling over her when she had walked into the room.

In that room, next to the wing chair, sat a round table hidden under a rich, full-skirted, red velvet cloth. Trimmed in an elegant gold fringe, it reached all the way to the floor, contrasting curiously with the worn carpet beneath it. And on this grand setting reposed a sparkling, crystal bowl holding the peppermints . . . tantalizing, tempting, pink-and-white-striped peppermint drops. The whole was a close cousin, if not an exact twin, to the one that had once sat in the parlor of Sugar Hill Hall! Had they been put there just for Emily's benefit? By whom? Certainly not by Mrs. Meeching or Mrs. Plumly, both now safely locked up in prison. By whom, then? Had those two . . . had they anything to do with "all"?

Sarah and Lucy's eyes flew wide open. "Peppermints?" they gasped together.

"Why?" asked Sarah.

"It—it has something to do with what happened to me before I came here," Emily replied, sitting up in her cot. "It's a long story, and later I'll tell it to you. But—but were they only just put there before I came?"

"Oh, no!" said Lucy. "They were there when we came months ago."

Months ago? Well, then, perhaps they had nothing to do with Emily alone, nothing to do with "all." But there still seemed something mysterious about it, something ominous. What?

Emily faltered. "Wh-Wh-Why are they there?" she asked.

"Mrs. Spilking tells you," said Sarah, and then paused to reconsider. "Well, she doesn't *exactly* tell you. It's like our stepmamas never *exactly* telling us why they don't want us. What her rule *says* is that the peppermints are there for guests only, and we're never to take one."

"Sarah and I have never seen a guest in the Front Room . . . not ever," Lucy said. "What we believe is that the peppermints are there for a temptation."

"It's no wonder," Sarah said, drawing her shoulders up and shuddering. "I wouldn't take one for my life! It's not like demerits, where what you get for punishment is mostly staying outside all alone when everyone else has come in, or extra lines in penmanship. And you have to have at least fifty demerits before you face dire consequences, the rules say. It only takes *one* peppermint to face them!"

"And we all know what dire consequences are," Lucy broke in, "because Mrs. Spilking always announces it when someone has to face them. It means the Cupboard!"

"Th-Th-The Cupboard?" stammered Emily. "Whatever is that?"

"It's a very tiny room in the cellar with a cot in it," replied Sarah. "When you get the Cupboard, it means spending the night there, with Wolf outside guarding the door just waiting to rip you to shreds!"

A very tiny room in the cellar with a cot in it! Was that not the very description of the grim Remembrance Room in Sugar Hill Hall? But terrible as that one was, it did not have a vicious dog posted outside that was panting to rip a person to shreds. Mrs. Spilking's Select Academy provided some very select horrors, indeed. And Emily had the prospect of facing them for more than five long years that seemed to be growing longer by the minute!

But now Sarah tugged anxiously at Lucy's arm. "We must go back down, Lucy. Mrs. Crumble will be here by now. We were only sent to look in on Emily, not to stay all day."

"Are you well enough to come with us?" Lucy asked Emily.

"I—I think so," replied Emily, climbing from her cot and managing to remain standing. "But who is Mrs. Crumble?"

"Mrs. Crumble comes in to watch over us while we do our embroidery and knitting and drawing, which we do mostly all day. She lives in a house nearby, she says. We expect she doesn't get paid much because she's Mrs. Spilking's sister. But she's nice, and we think she only pretends to be strict because she's as afraid of Mrs. Spilking as we are."

Well, it was certain that Mrs. Crumble did look very nice, indeed, sitting in the wing chair in the Front Room below. Her head was bent over an embroidery hoop, as were those of all the girls. Atop her head was a dainty lace doily, and perched on her nose was a pair of tiny spectacles. When Emily entered the room with Sarah and Lucy, she looked up to reveal blossom-pink cheeks and a tremulous smile. Sister to Mrs. Spilking she might be, but she appeared a far cry from Mrs. Spilking.

But did she not also present a picture as cozy as that presented by Mrs. Plumly when Emily first came through the doors of Sugar Hill Hall? And did Mrs. Plumly not turn out to be more evil, more treacherous, more wicked even than Mrs. Meeching, named "the snake lady" by Emily's friend Kipper, the fishmonger's boy? And, oh yes, had Mrs. Plumly, a splendid actress, not won Emily over by what turned out to be a totally false appearance of being terrified of Mrs. Meeching?

And there was Mrs. Crumble, sitting and smiling so sweetly, as if she were quite unaware of the table with the red velvet cloth and the sparkling bowl full of those deadly, seductive peppermints right beside her—quite unaware that anyone taking one would be led to a room in the cellar guarded by a dog that was fully prepared to tear a person to shreds.

So how was Emily to sit there calmly doing embroidery with fingers that had suddenly turned to lumps of ice? Well, she would do it, for she could pretend as well as anyone could. And while Sarah and Lucy and all the girls might think Mrs. Crumble was just as "nice" as she could be, Emily intended to be on her guard. For everything at Mrs. Spilking's Select Academy, including Mrs. Crumble, was whispering, *Beware, Emily Luccock. Beware!* And never for a moment forget . . .

"All"!

7

A Trip to the Cellar

"Watch your step. Ain't the best light down here," Bella warned as she led Emily by lantern light down the steep, narrow steps to the cellar. "And I been informed you're only to collect a clean nightdress and what goes on under the flippin' hew-nee-form. Anything else what might pass for pretty stays in the trunk. Hmmmph!" she snorted, passing judgment on this order.

Emily hesitated. "Is—is this where you have to live, Bella?"

"Where else?" said Bella with a shrug. "Servants' quarters is servants' quarters, and far as I know, the cellar is where they're mostly at."

Upon hearing this, Emily felt a sudden chill. When, after the evening meal, she had been attempting to learn to knit in the Front Room, with four lamps on the wall barely providing enough light to cast a shadow, she had been happy to be rescued by Bella, come on Mrs. Spilking's orders to fetch her to pay a visit to her trunk in the cellar. Now Emily wondered how she could have been so eager to come. Better to have remained in the Front Room learning to knit under the watchful eyes of Mrs. Crumble, struggling with impossibly long knitting needles, than to be where she was now.

Another cellar, oh so familiar, dank and dark, and heavy with the odors of mold and mildew! Servants' quarters! All reminders of her frightening introduction to Sugar Hill Hall! So what she must keep reminding herself now was that she was not a servant, that she did not have to live in a cellar, and most important of all, that she did not even have to stay at Mrs. Spilking's Select Academy forever, for she was still an heiress. Yes, an heiress possessed of an immense fortune!

"My room's that one," said Bella, once again putting her valuable thumb to use. "Over there's the laundry. Up front's the steps to the street what's used by me and Mrs. Slump. Trunk room's next building . . . this way."

Brushing aside dusty cobwebs, Bella now led Emily through a door into a small corridor matching the first. There was a door, as well, to steps leading out the front of the building.

"Where is the—the Cupboard?" Emily asked faintly, not entirely certain she really wanted to know.

"You heard about that already?" Bella asked. "Well, small wonder. Stuff like that gets 'round early on. Anyways, that's it." She jerked her head toward a closed door. "Always gives me the creeps just thinking 'bout it. Well, this here's the trunk room, and this trunk's the one got your name on it."

Bella leaned down and lifted up the lock of the trunk. "Hmmmph! Already been pried open, by Madam S., I presumes. No surprise why she never said you was to bring a key. Hope you ain't got anything in here you don't want her nose into."

Emily was all too familiar now with her trunks being broken into or even stolen in their entirety. She was actually happy to have her trunk even make an appearance. Quickly, she knelt down to unlatch and throw open the lid, with Bella holding the lantern over her head. It was clear that somebody had rifled through her belongings, but done so very carefully.

There was surely one thing Mrs. Spilking would have a great interest in finding. But when Emily looked at the place where Aunt Twice had carefully stitched in the two gold coins given her by Uncle Twice, she could see at once that the stitching had not been touched. Aunt Twice had done her work well!

And there was Abigail, the beautiful doll given her by Aunt and Uncle Twice! Emily picked her up and hugged her, but when she looked at Bella, Bella only shook her head and sighed. No, Abigail had to remain in the trunk. All Emily was to take from it, as Bella had said, was a nightdress and what she would wear under her gray uniform. Her red velveteen party dress, her navy blue sailor dress, and her green plaid skirt and yellow silk blouse must all remain behind. Without even pulling them out, Emily slipped her hands under each one, comforted in knowing they were there.

But what was that curious bundle she felt? It was hard, shaped like a flattened bottle, and in a thick wrapping of cotton cloth. If someone had not put their hand in just that exact spot, they might have missed it entirely. Emily pulled it out, carefully unwrapped the cloth, and then gasped. For what she found was, in truth, a bottle, flattened on opposite sides. On one side was pasted a label with somewhat rough, untidy printing: PA'S FISH SYRUP—TAKE IN CASE OF NEED. ALSO, TELL PIPER HELLO IF YOU EVER SEE HIM. KIPPER.

For a moment, Emily was too startled even to speak. How had Kipper managed to get this in her trunk? And then all at once, she remembered, and could hardly keep tears from springing into her eyes. Kipper had promised to send something along for her to remember him by when she left Sugar Hill Hall. Emily thought he had forgotten the promise, and with all that was happening to her, she had forgotten it herself . . . until now. Kipper must have secretly given it to Aunt Twice to slip into Emily's trunk, which, along with the gold coins, Aunt Twice had done most successfully.

"What in tarnation's that?" asked Bella, reading the label over Emily's shoulder. "Fish syrup! Ugh!"

"It isn't bad at all, really, Bella," Emily hurried to say. "It's something my friend Kipper's pa makes, to improve the appetite. And it works, too. I expect Mrs. Spilking didn't look carefully enough or she would have found it and then thrown it out. But, oh," Emily said wistfully, sighing. "I suppose I can't take it with me anyway."

"My eyesight ain't too good, and I ain't seen a thing," said Bella, pretending to gaze at the ceiling. "Wrap it up in your nightdress and bring it along. Just hide it good and proper in your room. Your appetite needs all the help it can get till you get used to Mrs. Slump's kwee-zeenee."

But it wasn't until Emily was back in her room and looking at the bottle once more that she puzzled over Kipper's message: "Tell Piper hello." Piper? Who was Piper? And then she remembered!

When Kipper's pa had left New York for San Francisco, his brother had stayed in New York. Piper was his brother's son, and therefore Kipper's cousin, although the boys had known each other only as babies. But Emily knew she had as much chance of meeting Piper to deliver the message as she had of making a trip to India . . . or the moon. She was a prisoner of Mrs. Spilking's Select Academy for Young Ladies, and that was that. Further, she could not even write Kipper to tell him she had the fish syrup, or write him anything at all. Just how would such a letter get past Mrs. Spilking? But at least Emily had the fish syrup. She would even share it with Sarah and Lucy, for Emily could see that their appetites needed improving as well, despite what they said.

So in the end, the trip to the cellar had proved worthwhile after all. Fish syrup! Seeing Abigail! Emily could hardly wait for Sarah and Lucy to leave the Front Room and come up to bed so she could make her report!

Emily's trip to the cellar turned out to be one of the happiest events of her long, dreary days at Mrs. Spilking's Select Academy. Even the friendship of Lucy and Sarah provided few happy moments, for they were both frightened of everything. Emily could not even persuade them to take more than a taste of the fish syrup. Oh, it was not that they thought it was unpleasant. It was because they actually were afraid Mrs. Spilking might catch a whiff of fish in case they should have to pass by her!

And how could Emily blame them? Mrs. Spilking's presence, whether or not seen, was felt everywhere, even when they lined up in the morning, shivering outside the bleak, icy washroom. For was she not waiting right below them in person to make certain no one was one moment late in arriving at the table? And was she not there to preside over the gray, tasteless, gluey lumps called "porridge" and to clear her throat threateningly if one extra grain of sugar found its way into a bowl?

It was also Mrs. Spilking who graced the noon table, where the girls were treated to slices of bread that had clearly departed a bakery days earlier, and that was hardly improved when spread with "butter" that was more likely pure lard, if color and flavor were any signs. Accompanying this tasty fare were cups of tea so weak they rivaled the milk that had come from the same pitcher that morning.

Needless to say, Mrs. Spilking also presided over the dinner table, where the same menu was provided day in and day out, potato and turnip stew, a dish as tasteless and unappetizing as the morning porridge. However, whereas the girls had to knit in the Front Room every night until bedtime in near darkness, Mrs. Spilking clearly believing money should not be wasted on anything so frivolous as eyesight, the food, such as it was, was always plentiful. It could only be concluded from this that girls were of no value to Mrs. Spilking if they perished from hunger, as then all payments from their families would perish with them.

In addition to the meals, Mrs. Spilking was also present to conduct the "class" in penmanship. She sat at the table with her eyes calculating not only what was being written, but also the amount of ink used to write it. One morning, one of the girls spilled two drops of ink as her pen traveled from the ink pot to her paper. Mrs. Spilking's eyes flared as she watched the poor offender try to mop up the spill with shaking hands, using a small rag of a handkerchief from her pocket.

"So," said Mrs. Spilking when this sad performance had ended, "it appears that Alicia has never learned the motto 'Waste not, want not' and has carelessly spilled valuable ink on the table. Alicia, would you like to repeat for the benefit of all rule number fifteen?"

"I-I-Ink spilled during penmanship, four demerits," recited Alicia, her pitifully thin, bent shoulders trembling.

"Very well," said Mrs. Spilking, instantly opening the black notebook on the table before her. With lips compressed into a tight, disapproving line, she found the right page in the book, and *tick-tick-tick-ticked* on it with her pen. "Hmm, that makes twelve demerits, all for the same misdemeanor! Tomorrow morning, Alicia, you will stay behind to provide me with thirty copies of that rule in perfect penmanship, with *no* drops of spilled ink!"

After this pronouncement, Mrs. Spilking treated everyone at the table to a flare of her eyes, and then proceeded to narrow them. "Perhaps it is now time for another rule review. It has been several days since the last one, and we don't want to forget them, do we?"

Each girl at the table dutifully shook her head, as who there would have dared to do otherwise?

"All right, then," said Mrs. Spilking. "Adelaide, rule number nine, if you will?"

"Being late for breakfast, three demerits," replied Adelaide in a nervous rush of words.

Mrs. Spilking then waited a few moments, allowing her gaze to move around the table, resting briefly on each girl as if she were to be the next victim. "Rule number three . . ." Her eyes snapped back to a girl she had just passed. "Imogene?"

"T-T-Taking too long in the washroom, four demerits," quavered Imogene.

"Rule number nineteen, Eudora," said Mrs. Spilking so quickly that it caught the next victim off guard.

"I—I—I—," stammered Eudora, swallowing and swallowing, unable to go on.

"Perhaps, Emily, you would like to help Eudora?" said Mrs. Spilking. "She seems to have lost her voice. I hope you have yours."

Emily hesitated. Oh, it was not because she did not know the rule. With the help of Sarah and Lucy, she knew them all by now, backward and forward. So, undoubtedly, did Eudora, had she not been taken so by surprise. Now the look of fear and desperation on her face almost made Emily want to "forget" the rule as well, out of sympathy for a fellow student in such misery.

"Well?" Mrs. Spilking's sharp finger tapped on the table. Her eyes glistened as she anticipated the collapse of another victim.

"Wasting thread in embroidery, three demerits," Emily rattled off, for any thoughts of "forgetting" the rule in support of Eudora's feelings would have been quite mad, and accomplished nothing.

But with this moment of triumph denied to her, Mrs. Spilking lost no time in returning to pounce on her earlier prey.

"Now, Eudora, having failed with rule number nineteen, perhaps you would care to enlighten us with your knowledge of rule number one?"

"F-F-Failure to know the rules by heart, ten demerits," replied Eudora in a fading voice.

"Quite right! And don't you think you then deserve what I am about to enter in my demerit book?" inquired Mrs. Spilking with all the sincerity of a fox asking the opinion of the hen he is about to make his next meal.

Eudora's head now hung so low, she was barely able to nod.

With a great flourish of her pen, Mrs. Spilking *tick-ticked* Eudora's demerits into her black book, and the inquisition continued. When at last it had ended, Mrs. Spilking reminded them it was letter-writing day. So Emily, after all the misery of what had just transpired, had to write Aunt and Uncle Twice her usual letter telling them how much she continued to love being at Mrs. Spilking's Select Academy. She still, of course, had not received any letter at all from them.

But, oh, how she would like to have been able to tell them of the dismal, dreary days marching by, one exactly like the other. Mornings spent with embroidery and mending; afternoons spent with more embroidery; drawing, in which they took pencils and tablets from their boxes and drew with no instruction whatsoever; grammar, in which they simply studied ancient grammar books entirely on their own; and reading from deadly dull books so dilapidated their covers were all but falling off.

These "lessons" were interrupted only by the horrible meals, by a one-hour nap in bed in the afternoon with all conversation forbidden, and by two grim "exercise" periods, where they were required to march around and around a small, barren patch of ground called a "garden," but where surely no daffodil, daisy, or rose had ever bloomed. There they were not allowed even to whisper to one another but had to march in silence to the accompaniment of a barking dog. For in the very same amount of small space allotted the girls, separated from them by a brick wall, was the space allotted to Mrs. Spilking's vicious dog, Wolf!

And though, excepting meals, penmanship, and

letter writing, not to mention the rule inquisitions, it was Mrs. Crumble who watched over the girls, still, who was to know when Mrs. Spilking might suddenly appear in person?

One morning, having spied from a rear window, she arrived in the "garden" to accuse two girls of whispering. Four demerits each! And on another never-to-be-forgotten afternoon, she rushed out to ask a girl to place in her handkerchief something she had been seen putting in her mouth. Mrs. Spilking passed the offending object under her pinched nose, sniffing suspiciously.

"What is this?" she inquired. "Do I detect the odor of peppermint?"

"A—A—A cough drop I've been saving since I came here," replied the girl, looking as if she might faint. "I—I—I have a sore throat."

"Well, take it, then!" said Mrs. Spilking coldly, in no way able to equate the dark little lump in the handkerchief with a forbidden pink-and-white-striped peppermint. "See that it does you some good!"

Oh, yes, Mrs. Spilking's presence was everywhere! It was no wonder the girls were all so quiet, and wore such sad faces most of the time.

For what did any of them have to look forward to but more of the same dreary days, all with the frightening specter of Mrs. Spilking hovering over them? For Emily, it would come to an end when she came into her fortune, but the five and more years continued to look longer and longer to her.

The only girl there who did not appear sad and forlorn was Princess Delilla. And why should she? She clearly had nothing to fear from Mrs. Spilking, and did not even have to learn the rules, much less mind them. She could get up and walk out during embroidery or grammar or penmanship, with neither Mrs. Spilking nor Mrs. Crumble saying a word to her about it. She never even bothered to take part in the "exercise" periods. Let other girls parade around the barren yard with the icy wind freezing their noses. She simply took her aristocratic one up the stairs and disappeared into her room.

Well, as the girls all sat in the Front Room working, had not Emily often looked through the open door into the hallway and seen Mrs. Spilking accompanied by the princess parade down the hall and out the front door? Then had they not returned carrying boxes and full shopping bags?

Exercise in the backyard, indeed! Why should the princess bother with that when she could have her exercise in such other pleasant ways?

As for food, "her royal majestry" simply picked at that, and yet she managed to look perfectly healthy and well fed. Emily, it must be said, was not terribly surprised. She remembered how Bella had remarked on Mrs. Spilking sharing the precious little frosted cakes with "her royal majestry." And no doubt other delicious food was shared with her, as well: fresh fruit, cheese, and butter from the grocer's, freshly baked bread and cakes from the baker's. It was certain Princess Delilla did not have to rely on Mrs. Slump's kitchen for her nourishment any more than Mrs. Spilking did.

The princess could not have had more attention paid to her in her royal palace in her own country, wherever that was. Sarah and Lucy often said that Mrs. Spilking's academy was as much a palace for her as her own in that mysterious country. And Emily would have been hard put to disagree with that!

In the meanwhile, the dreary days went on. And on. And on. Would there be no end to them?

8

A Royal Favor

They had just come in from morning exercise when Emily decided she needed a visit to the washroom. She raised her hand, made her request, and was given permission by Mrs. Crumble to leave. Laying down her embroidery hoop, Emily hurried to the door, only to realize that Princess Delilla had stood up and was following right behind her. The princess, of course, never had to receive permission for much of anything. She just came and went as she chose. Emily thought nothing of it.

When they reached the top of the stairs, she turned to go to her washroom, and the princess turned in the opposite direction. Whether she went to her room or not, Emily did not know, nor for that matter much cared. But what she did know was that when she left the washroom, Princess Delilla was standing at the head of the stairs, waiting. As soon as she caught sight of Emily, she beckoned to her. At the same time she put a finger to her lips, a sign for Emily to keep quiet. Tiptoeing to her room, she signaled Emily to follow her.

Now, although Emily had once or twice caught Princess Delilla staring at her in a calculating manner, she had believed that the princess probably stared at the other girls in the same way. Now she was not so certain. Princess Delilla clearly had something in mind for her all along. The question was ... what?

The princess closed the door very carefully and softly behind them as soon as they entered the room. And what a room it was! Why, it was impossible to believe that there even *was* such a room at Mrs. Spilking's Select Academy, especially considering the rooms in which all the other girls lived.

"Nice, isn't it?" said Princess Delilla with an indifferent shrug.

Nice? Why, it was so startlingly nice that Emily could do no more than nod as she looked around the room with wide eyes. In it was a proper bed complete with carved walnut posters, not the iron cots enjoyed by everyone else. On the bed were piles of pillows and a puffy down comforter with a cover of pale pink rosebuds. Rosebuds twined in profusion in a painted frieze that reached all around the walls. And there was more.

Against one wall, in addition to a handsome, gleaming chest of drawers, was a dainty, mirrored dressing table. And as if a round, pink wool rug were not enough to warm the floor, beside the bed where the princess would first put her royal toes in the morning lay a white bearskin rug. On the tops of the chest and dressing table sat pretty little china dishes and figurines beside displays of photographs in silver frames—without doubt, photographs of the princess's royal family.

But the centerpiece of the room was a delightful slipper chair in pink velveteen. Beside it was set a small, round walnut table holding a flowered glass oil lamp and a pink china bowl.

"Would you like one?" Princess Delilla asked.

Emily felt her face grow hot, for she realized she had been staring at the china bowl. It was heaped with an assortment of delectable fancy biscuits. For a moment, she was in such a state of confusion, she could not reply.

"Go ahead, take one!" said the princess. "Lots more where that came from. Go on! I won't tell."

"Th-th-thank you, but I'd better not, Your— Your Royal Highness," stammered Emily.

"Whyever not?" asked Princess Delilla. "And you may call me 'Princess.' That's good enough."

"Thank you, P-P-Princess, but I . . . I *must* get back downstairs," said Emily.

"Oh, no. What you *must* do is stay here for a few more minutes," said Princess Delilla airily. "I didn't invite you in just to visit my room, you know."

Well, of course she had not! Did the princess really believe Emily was so stupid as to think that? Not knowing what she was expected to say to that, however, Emily remained silent as the princess made a big pretense of choosing a biscuit, while stealing a glance sideways with her cat-green eyes to see what Emily had made of her revelation.

"I have something I want you to do for me," she said, taking a nibble from her biscuit. "I expect you could call it a favor. It isn't much, really. I could ask one of the other girls, but I don't fancy asking the older ones, and the younger ones like you always look so frightened. I've been watching you, and I've decided you're much smarter and braver than they are. So now, would you like to know what the favor is?"

Though she could not help but be curious, Emily was not at all certain she *did* want to know. Somehow, she did not like the sound of any of this. The princess had indeed been studying her all along, just as she suspected. But what had she done to make the princess think she was brave and smart? Nothing, that was what! Was it not more likely that she had been selected because she was new in the school, and also a younger girl who could be easily twisted around a wily older girl's finger? Was not being told she was smart and brave only an attempt to butter her up?

What she should do, then, was simply call the princess's bluff by thanking her for the great honor bestowed upon her, but then politely state that she was not as smart and brave as the princess supposed, and prove it by saying how frightened she was to stay any longer. Then she would quickly escape the room.

But it was easier to think all this than come out and say it when the cat eyes of a member of royalty were staring right through her. Emily's thoughts, all neatly strung out in her head, instantly fell into disarray. And almost before she was quite aware of what she was doing, she found herself nodding her head.

"Good!" Princess Delilla pounced with lightning speed. "I knew you would! But first, I must tell you it has to do with chocolate. Now, that's not so bad, is it . . . chocolate?"

"Ch-Ch-Chocolate?" stammered Emily. The princess was right. What could be bad about chocolate? Oh, but there must be more than that. The princess had dropped the first shoe. There *must* be a second yet to be dropped, but what could it possibly be?

"Yes, chocolate!" repeated Princess Delilla. "You see, I *love* chocolate. I truly *long* for chocolate. Only Mrs. Spilking won't let me have any."

"But Mrs. Spilking lets you have anything you want, doesn't she?" asked Emily, and then threw a hand to her mouth in horror at her boldness in having said this. What would a princess have to say to such rudeness from a mere commoner?

Not much, it appeared, for she had more important things on her mind. "Not chocolate," she said. "Mrs. Spilking won't let me have that. She says it would spoil my complexion. She believes she has a sacred trust placed upon her by my family not to let that or other disagreeable things happen to me. So, that's what my favor is . . . to get me some chocolate!"

Well, the second shoe had now been dropped. Emily was to get the chocolate!

"How—how am I to do that?" she asked.

"Weeell," drawled the princess with a sly look at Emily, "when you leave the school and go left for two blocks, there's Binkwig's Grocers. That's where the chocolate—I mean, *chocolates*—are."

"But—but I'm not allowed to leave the school," said Emily faintly.

"Oh, I *know*," said Princess Delilla, looking at her with the greatest sympathy. "But I have it all worked out. It will be easy. I heard Mrs. Spilking telling Bella she would be away until late this afternoon. All you have to do is slip out the front door at nap time, leave the door unlocked while you run and fetch my chocolates, and then slip right back in again."

All Emily had to do! It would be easy! Was the princess mad? Why, there were all sorts of things that would not make it easy at all.

"What about Sarah and Lucy, my roommates?"

asked Emily. "What shall I say to them if they ask where I'm going?"

"Just say you're going to the washroom," replied the princess airily. "They're supposed to be sleeping anyway, and not asking questions, aren't they?"

"Oh, Princess!" cried Emily. "Why is it *you* can't go?"

"Because," said Princess Delilla, "despite what you think about me being allowed everything, I'm not allowed out either, unless I'm with Mrs. Spilking. Besides, Mr. Binkwig knows me, as I've been there often with Mrs. Spilking. He'd report to her in a minute."

"But he'd know I was a Spilking Academy girl from my uniform, and report that as well!" said Emily, desperately grasping at reasons why she should not go on this errand.

"Not if you're wearing your coat and bonnet," said the princess coolly.

Now Emily could think of but one more reason. Fortunately, it was the best yet and should surely end the matter: "How can I buy chocolates?" she said. "I have no money. We're not allowed to have any."

"Oh, I've thought of that. Here!" replied

Princess Delilla, and whipped an envelope out of her pocket. "Take this with you. It's a note requesting a sack of chocolates, the ones Mr. Binkwig keeps in a glass case. But whatever you do"—the princess paused to look hard at Emily—"*whatever you do*, do *not* give this note to Mr. Binkwig. He'll report both of us to Mrs. Spilking if you do. Mr. Binkwig is short and fat and bald and wears an apron, so you'll know who he is. What you're to do is give it to the grocer's boy. The grocer's boy will wear an apron as well, but he's tall and thin and has dark hair and is much, much younger. He knows me well, too, but he won't say a word to anyone. He'll sneak the chocolates, and nobody will know. Now, is that all clear?"

Oh, very clear, indeed, and very clearly something Emily most certainly did not wish to do. But she had been artfully led into agreeing to it by a very cunning, crafty girl who happened to be a member of royalty held in the highest esteem by Mrs. Spilking. If Emily were to back out now, who could know what misery the princess might arrange for her later? Better to do what she had agreed to and be done with it.

If only Mrs. Crumble had sent someone to look

for her. After all, Emily had been missing for more time than it took to visit the washroom. But Mrs. Crumble must have been dozing, as she often did. So Emily had not been sent for, and now there was no escape. She must do the "favor" for the princess.

Princess Delilla—"her royal majestry"—so spoiled, so bent on having her own way, and so very, very clever in arranging it! Princess Delilla, who was perfectly willing to put a young girl at risk all because she had to have chocolates! And it was "smart" and "brave" Emily who was the lucky one chosen to get them for her!

9

A Deadly Surprise

Emily continued to hope that some miracle would happen to keep her from the frightening trip to Binkwig's Grocers for Princess Delilla's chocolates. But no miracle *did* happen. She had even thought it might be possible to stumble during exercise period and injure an ankle, but she had been unable to manage that. No, the minutes simply marched safely by. Even Sarah and Lucy, always dutifully obeying every rule to the letter, had their eyes snapped so tightly shut Emily easily tiptoed from the room without a murmur from either of them.

Then there she was, her heart thumping, creeping down the stairs, fetching her coat and bonnet from the dining room, and then quietly letting herself out the front door. It was possible Bella might have made an entry into the hall as Emily slipped from the building, and successfully put a stop to the whole venture. But even that did not happen. She was on the street with nothing at all that could then come between herself and Binkwig's Grocers. Drawing in a deep breath, she began her journey.

Fear made her want to run, but she knew running might attract attention, so she simply walked as fast as she could down the street. The store, just as the princess had said, was only two blocks away, and so it was but minutes before Emily was cautiously opening the glass door with BINKWIG'S printed on it in bold black letters.

What if Mr. Binkwig presented himself to wait on her? What was she to do? But to her intense relief, the short, fat, bald man in the apron was already busy waiting on another customer, and someone else was in line to be waited on by him. The tall, thin young man was at work on a ladder, rearranging tin cans on a shelf in the back of the store. Pretending to examine the other shelves, Emily sidled up to the ladder. When the young man caught sight of her staring up at him, he quickly climbed down. Before he even had a chance to speak, Emily silently handed him the envelope. He opened it and read the note at once.

"Right this way, miss," he said when he had finished it. Princess Delilla was entirely right. There was going to be no problem with this young man, that was now certain.

Well, it was hardly surprising. The princess was very pretty and was royalty as well. This was an enticing combination, and the young man had no doubt been smitten with her when she had accompanied Mrs. Spilking to the store. The princess, likewise no doubt, was quite aware of this and knew she could count on him to keep a secret.

Mr. Binkwig was so busy with his customers, and yet a third coming into the store, that he paid no attention to what was going on at the glass case that held the chocolates. There the young man carefully lifted some out with a tin scoop and poured them into a small, brown paper sack. Then he handed the sack to Emily.

"Tell her I hope she enjoys them," he said with a broad smile.

So nervous she could barely smile back, Emily hurried from the store, clutching the bag tightly against herself. Then she hurried back to the school, flew up the front steps, and with shaking fingers, twisted the door handle. It would not turn, which could only mean . . . No, oh no, the front door was locked! She rattled the handle. How was she ever to get in the building? Must she remain on the steps waiting for Mrs. Spilking to return and let her in? Terrified, she rattled the handle again. The door remained tightly shut. Well, she could ring the bell, and Bella would answer it and very likely ask no questions. There would be the end of it.

But before Emily could even raise her hand to ring the bell, she heard a key being turned in the lock inside. The door slowly opened to reveal someone standing behind it, someone in a gray dress who was wearing keys on a dull brass ring dangling from a narrow black belt. And Emily found herself staring, like a rabbit caught in the glaring light of a carriage lamp, directly into the flaring eyes of Mrs. Spilking!

"So now I know why it was that I returned to find the front door unlocked!" she said, coldly furious. "I looked out my office window, and what did I see flying down the street but one of my

Select Academy girls, and the newest one at that. And what have we here?"

Mrs. Spilking snatched the paper sack from Emily and peered into it. "Chocolates! I see. The food here is not good enough for you or plentiful enough for you, so you must sneak out when I am away to purchase chocolates at the grocer's. And may I ask, Miss Luccock, how you were able to purchase these when it is clearly stated in the rules that girls are not allowed to have money?"

"Oh, but I *didn't* buy them!" cried Emily.

Mrs. Spilking threw a hand to her throat as if gasping for air. "That can only mean, then, that you *stole* them! Worse and worse!"

"But I didn't steal them!" Emily was now almost hysterical. "I *didn't!*"

"So then," said Mrs. Spilking, "you didn't buy them, nor did you steal them. I suppose someone in the store simply *gave* them to you? Is that what you're expecting me to believe?"

"But—but someone *did!*" Emily replied with a sob. "I had a note from the princess to the young man. *She* wanted the chocolates and—"

"*What?*" Mrs. Spilking's eyes flared again with burning rage as she drew her face close to Emily's.

"Are you now trying to tell me that the princess had something to do with this? Well, we shall see about it. You will please follow me!" she snapped. Then, turning, she marched angrily up the stairs.

Emily trailed after her in total misery and horror. For in very truth, she would never have intentionally revealed to anyone what the princess had asked of her, and certainly not to Mrs. Spilking. Emily had decided she did not care much for Princess Delilla, and she knew the princess had taken unfair advantage of her. Still, she also knew this was a secret, and as she had agreed to do the favor, it followed that she must keep the secret . . . she must keep the pledge.

Could she ever make the princess understand how Mrs. Spilking had led her right into breaking it? Could the princess realize how terrified she had been when Mrs. Spilking had met her at the door when she returned with the chocolates? Not keeping a secret, breaking a pledge made to royalty was unthinkable. Emily had done this, but she would try in every way to make it up to the princess. In every *possible* way!

Emily had once heard Uncle Twice use the expression "noblesse oblige." When she had asked about it, he had explained that it meant the honorable, generous, responsible behavior associated with high rank or birth. So there was no question about Princess Delilla admitting to her part in this wrongdoing. There was, of course, no way that she could keep Emily from most surely receiving some kind of punishment, although it might be nothing worse than a few extra demerits if the princess pleaded her case. The princess would, happily, receive only a slight scolding from Mrs. Spilking, and be warned again about the evils of chocolate in regard to her complexion. And there it would all end. Still, Emily was trembling when they were admitted to the princess's room.

"I am sorry that we must disturb your nap time, Princess," Mrs. Spilking began at once. "I have been told a story by Emily Luccock, standing here before you, which I do not believe for one moment. She claims to have had a note from you to a young man at a store requesting that he give you chocolates. That would be Binkwig's Grocers, I presume."

"I have no idea what you're talking about, Mrs. Spilking," said Princess Delilla, looking Emily dead in the eye without so much as blinking.

"Then you never did write such a note?" inquired Mrs. Spilking.

"Absolutely not!" replied the princess coldly. "I would never do that, or go hunting for chocolates when you have forbidden me to have any. How would anyone dare to say such a thing?"

"Well, *somebody* did!" said Mrs. Spilking, turning to Emily with a look of triumph. "And this behavior certainly deserves an appropriate reward, which I intend to announce when we return downstairs. Would you care to be present, Princess?"

"I don't believe so," the princess replied with a shrug. "I'm sure you will deal with this in any way you think best." Her cat eyes had no expression in them whatsoever as she watched Emily leave the room with Mrs. Spilking.

Nap time had ended, and the girls were all back in their places in the Front Room. Emily was still in her coat and bonnet, with a sharp finger in her back propelling her forward to notify her that she was to continue with Mrs. Spilking to the head of the room, where Mrs. Crumble now sat.

"You are to remain standing and facing the girls, Emily," ordered Mrs. Spilking. "Girls, please put down your work. I have something of extreme importance to announce, and it requires your full attention."

In a moment, the slight rustling that attended the laying down of embroidery hoops ended. The room now fell so silent it almost seemed as if no one was even breathing.

"Girls," began Mrs. Spilking, her eyes traveling around the room, fixing on each, one by one. "You see here before you someone in a coat and bonnet, the coat and bonnet she was wearing when she left the school with *no permission from anyone!*"

Her eyes flaring, Mrs. Spilking waited a suitable length of time for this shocking news to settle before continuing. "But this is not her only crime, for there are worse to come. Do you see this?" She raised her arm, dangling in front of her the brown paper sack she had continued holding. "Chocolates! It contains *chocolates!* Not content with the food so generously provided by our Select Academy, Miss Luccock has seen fit to avail herself of chocolates from the grocer's. And not even purchased with forbidden money, which is bad enough, but stolen, girls, *stolen!*"

Mrs. Spilking snapped the sack down by her

side as her lips tightened to an angry, pencil-thin line. "Compounding this crime," she continued in a deadly, low voice, as if the next was too terrible to be uttered aloud, "she has lied . . . *lied* about it. And, worse yet, she has attempted to place the blame on someone else. Yes, on someone else . . . our very own princess, the Princess Delilla, who honors us by gracing our Select Academy with her presence!"

If the looks on the girls' faces had gone from dread at the words "someone else" to relief at hearing that the blame had been placed on the princess, lest someone in that room be called upon to defend herself, Mrs. Spilking was happily too intent on describing Emily's wickedness to notice. She relentlessly drove on.

"So it appears that we have here someone who has broken one of our most sacred rules, has stolen, lied, and ended by accusing an innocent person of her crimes." Mrs. Spilking drew herself up, pursed her lips, and flared her eyes, waiting for this list of horrors to be registered and perma- nently recorded by all present. It was clear that she was now approaching the high point of this trial.

"And now I ask you . . . I ask *each* of you what

you think might be a suitable punishment for all this, bearing in mind that not one but four . . . *four* crimes have been committed, some of which are of such magnitude they are not even on our rule list!"

If anyone in the room had any ideas along these lines, it was certain she would not have suggested them for her life. So, needless to say, nobody raised a hand, nor, also needless to say, had Mrs. Spilking expected anyone to do so. The very room itself seemed to stop breathing when she turned to the bowl of peppermints, delicately picked one up with long, white, bony fingers, toyed with it a moment, and then let it slide back through her fingers into the bowl.

"Well, then, I *do* have an idea," she said silkily. "It seems to me that a basket of four such crimes is worth at least as much as one peppermint. And so, I must sentence her to our beloved Select Academy's most extreme punishment. One guilty of such wickedness should pay the price as others have done for far lesser crimes.

"Therefore, you, Emily Luccock, will remain here until the evening meal, of which, out of the kindness of my heart, you will be allowed to partake. You will then return here for the remainder

of the evening. When, however, the other girls prepare to retire to their rooms, you will be led by me
from this room to the cellar stairs. You will descend
those stairs as other culprits have done, be led
through the door and down the corridor to ... the
Cupboard. There you will remain under the guard
of my dog, Wolf, until I come for you in the
morning."

The Cupboard! Emily had thought she was
being so clever with her glowing letters to India,
making a big show under Mrs. Spilking's watchful
eye of never taking a grain more than the allotted
amount of sugar on her porridge, and not only
minding every rule, but knowing them so well
that she could have recited them in her sleep. Yet
"smart" Emily Luccock had somehow managed to
get herself sentenced to the "beloved" Select
Academy's most extreme punishment.

She had clearly failed in "smartness." Would she
fail in "bravery" as well? She had survived the horrors of the Remembrance Room, but how much
bravery was required to sleep near a dog that was
prepared to rip you to shreds? How was she ever
to survive *that*?

10

The Cupboard

There was *something* there. In the suffocating darkness and deep silence, unbroken by even a whisper of air, Emily knew there was *something*. And it was right outside her door! There was no other sound but that, for the creaking of footsteps overhead had long since stopped. Now there was no sound but that one, the one outside the door.

She knew something was there because Mrs. Spilking said there would be. And if Emily had had any doubts about it, they came to a sudden end when earlier she had heard the door to the corridor open and then close. This was followed by whining and scratching on that door. When this proved fruitless, there came the sounds of metal chinking up and down the corridor, and then that, too, ended. For a while there was silence, and then

Emily began to hear the sounds outside the door.

She lay in the small room, rigid as the cot under her, staring at the ceiling. Sleep was impossible. Every time she closed her eyes, ghostly shadows flitted across her eyelids. And it seemed that the thoughts she could not keep away only became worse when her eyes were shut.

She had determined that she *would* be brave. And so she had managed to be when Mrs. Spilking had marched her down to the Cupboard. After all, she had been marched to the Remembrance Room by Mrs. Meeching, and so was experienced in such marches. Lucy and Sarah would have been in tears. Emily had marched out dry eyed and with her jaw set. Brave Emily! Well, her bravery had all melted away in the dark cellar room! Even the Remembrance Room, after all, did not have something outside the door waiting, perhaps even hoping, to rip her to shreds. Emily was not simply frightened now. She was terrified!

What would Aunt and Uncle Twice think if they knew of this? Would they not be angry, and repent at having so carelessly left her in such a horror of a place? But they never would know— not while they were in India, at any rate. For

Emily must go right on writing them the same cheerful letters reporting how much she loved being at Mrs. Spilking's Select Academy for Young Ladies, just as she had been doing every week. And yet so far, she had still not heard from them. Not one single word!

And what of the girls who had listened to Mrs. Spilking's accusations? Four terrible crimes! Did they really believe she had committed them? And, oh, most particularly, did Sarah and Lucy believe it? She had not had a moment to talk with them before her sentence was carried out, as the only time they ever had for conversations, albeit the very shortest imaginable, was just before they went to bed at night. Further, everyone had kept their eyes cast down in front of her, as if frightened to be seen looking at her. Emily Luccock, arch criminal! And defiant, as well. Perhaps she *should* have shed tears . . . tears of repentance. But, no, she had had to be Emily the brave. If they could but see her now!

As for the princess, Emily traveled back and forth between a state of terror and a state of rage. That Princess Delilla! Noblesse oblige, indeed! What country did she come from that she had never been taught the meaning of those words? Well, Emily must remember never, never to visit it. And if she did, she would certainly visit the palace and express her opinion about it. Her opinion about it . . . her opinion about it . . . the palace . . . the palace . . . girls think of her . . . think of her . . . Lucy and Sarah . . . Lucy and Sarah . . . Emily's thoughts were getting more and more muddled, as at long last, she drifted into a troubled sleep. And sometime during the night, she had a dream.

It was a terrible dream. She was in a tiny boat, all alone, rowing and rowing, but all the while staying in one place. Somewhere way ahead of her, masked by a thick fog, were two people. She could not tell who they were, but she knew she must reach them. Keep rowing, keep rowing, harder and harder. And then, the waves began to swell in front of her, and heavy spray washed over her face. It washed and it washed and would not stop. Suddenly, she woke with a start. But the washing went on. *Slosh! Slosh! Slosh!* Right over her chin and the tip of her nose.

The washing had not stopped with her dream, but what did almost stop, in truth, was Emily's heart. For the washing came from a very large, very wet tongue! Emily lay absolutely motionless, stiff with fear, and hardly breathing. The licking continued, and then something came over the side of her cot and began determinedly pawing at her shoulder. It took very little thinking on Emily's part to realize that this was the dog. This was Wolf! The door to the Cupboard must not have been tightly closed, and he had succeeded in pushing his way in.

But his actions were hardly those of a dog who had entered with the idea of ripping her to shreds. No, he gave every sign of wishing to be friends— and to get petted in the bargain! Emily drew in a deep breath and held it as she shakily reached out a hand and began to scratch behind a big, floppy, velvet-smooth ear.

"G-G-Good boy!" she whispered.

The "good boy" whined his approval and flopped his large head down beside her on the hard mattress with a sigh of contentment.

So this was Wolf, who, thanks to Mrs. Spilking, was held in such dread by all the girls. Suddenly, Emily now realized that although she had heard him barking behind the fence and accompanying Mrs. Spilking on her nightly bed checks, she had never actually seen him again after she had arrived at the academy that first night. At that time, of course, he had only been exhibited to her attached to a heavy black chain held tightly by Mrs. Spilking in a most ominous way. Could the way she was holding him be the reason he had growled? At any rate, it was more than likely the other girls had not had personal encounters with Wolf, either, so knew as little about him as Emily did.

It appeared that Wolf's interest in ripping anyone to shreds was simply a clever invention of Mrs. Spilking's cruel mind, which rippled through the school, spreading terror as it went. Why, Wolf was no more threatening than Clarabelle, the kitten that Kipper had brought to Emily, and that had ended up brightening the lives of the old people at Sugar Hill Hall.

Only now Emily was presented with a dilemma. If Wolf remained by her cot, and Mrs. Spilking were to find him there in the morning, she would know that her deception had been discovered. What terrible things might she invent to take its place? Emily must do something about this.

"Good boy!" she whispered again, and while continuing to rub Wolf's ear, cautiously put one foot on the floor, and then the other.

"Come along, boy! Come along, Wolf!" Emily said, taking the dog by his collar and gently tugging on it.

He padded right along with her as she felt for the door in the dark. It was open, just as she had suspected, and she led the dog through it.

"Good boy! Down!" Emily said. Although they were in total darkness, she could sense that he had dropped to the floor. "Good boy! Now stay!" she said, and with one last rub behind his ear, she stepped back into the Cupboard, closed the door, and climbed back onto the hard cot.

Emily was thoroughly pleased with herself for remembering how her papa had trained the dog they once had, for repeating the words he had used. But more than that, think of it, Wolf such a gentle dog and now lying quietly outside the door! She could only hope that if she ever did encounter him with Mrs. Spilking, he would not wag his tail and reveal their secret. It was a good thing she made her bed checks in the near dark and was less able to see a tail wagging! That was the last thing Emily remembered thinking before she fell into a deep and dreamless sleep.

• • •

"Sarah and I never did believe you'd done all those things!" declared Lucy.

It was the next night, and they were in their room before bedtime. Now Emily could finally have the conversation that would explain all that had happened to her.

"That princess! How could she tell such a lie!" Sarah was furious. "How *could* she, an actual member of a royal family!"

"Well, we all know she doesn't care about anyone but herself," said Lucy, scowling. "You can tell. Sending you into such danger just because she fancies chocolates. I wish you'd got them for her, Emily, and she'd broken out all over in spots. I do, indeed. Serve her right!"

"But, oh, Lucy and Sarah," cried Emily, "what of the other girls? Do you think they believe everything Mrs. Spilking said about me?"

Sarah and Lucy exchanged glances. "We don't know," replied Sarah. "But what we believe they think is that if you really did what she said, you're about the bravest girl they know, and they wish they'd had the courage."

"It's what Sarah and I thought, anyway," said Lucy, with an eager bob of her head. Then she added quickly in great confusion, "I mean, it's what we *would* have thought if we didn't really believe you hadn't done those things."

"And we do think you were so brave being led to the Cupboard without even crying," said Sarah. "I expect you'll be the school heroine, though no one would ever dare say so."

"But, oh, that Cupboard!" Lucy clasped her hands together in anguish. "How did you bear it? Sarah and I would have perished."

"Oh, yes!" agreed Sarah, moaning. "We would indeed have with that—that horrible dog just aching to rip us to shreds. How were you able to sleep listening to him panting his hot breath outside your door? Didn't you just faint dead away?" Both girls threw their arms around themselves and shuddered.

Now, Emily had not been at all certain that she should tell them about Wolf. She desperately wanted to, but she knew that the more people who knew a secret, the less likely it was to remain a secret. But it was rapidly becoming unbearable, not telling what she knew about Wolf when she saw the looks on Sarah's and Lucy's faces.

"He wasn't outside my door," Emily blurted. "He was right inside the room!"

Lucy and Sarah both gasped, looking as if *they* were the ones who were going to faint dead away. Emily, who had no intention of frightening them so, rushed on breathlessly.

"Oh, it was all right, really it was! He managed to push open the door, which turned out not to be closed tightly. But all he wanted was to be petted! He came over to my cot and put his head down beside me. So I scratched his ear, and he was as content as could be. I don't believe he has ever wanted to rip anyone to shreds in his life. Mrs. Spilking has been lying about him to frighten us to death!"

"Well, she has!" declared Lucy. Then she hesitated. "Did—did he stay with you all night?"

"No, I couldn't let him do that," explained Emily. "I knew he shouldn't be there when Mrs. Spilking came to fetch him in the morning. So I just led him out, and he lay down like a lamb. Then I closed the door and went back to my cot and went to sleep."

"Oh, Emily, I wish all the girls could know," said Sarah wistfully. "I wish we could find a way to tell them."

"Oh, no! No! No! You mustn't even think about it!" cried Emily. "Mrs. Spilking must never know what I found out. It's too dangerous, and the more people who know about it, the more likely it is she'll find out. I was even afraid to tell *you* about it!"

"But we're so glad you did!" exclaimed Lucy. "And I don't care what you say, you must have been scared out of your wits when Wolf came in. I still think you're the bravest girl ever!"

"I do too!" echoed Sarah. "And even if we can't say anything about Wolf, I do know what I *am* going to say. I intend to whisper to someone during exercise about how you did *not* do all those terrible things that Mrs. Spilking said you did. So . . . so there!"

"You'll do no such thing, Sarah!" ordered Emily, hearing the quaver in Sarah's voice. "Some day they're sure to find out one way or another, and all you'll do is get demerits for whispering. Say you won't do it?"

"Well, all right," agreed a clearly relieved Sarah. "I promise I won't."

"But if we don't get into bed right away," said Emily, "we'll be caught when Mrs. Spilking comes around on her bed check."

"But just think," said Lucy. "For the first time since I've been here, I won't be trembling, wondering if I might be the one ripped to shreds!"

"Oh, Emily," Sarah said breathlessly, "nor will I!"

The looks they gave Emily came very close to making up for all of it. Nobody in that room would have anything to fear from Wolf ever again. Wolf, who would no more rip anyone to shreds than . . . than Clarabelle. Yes, it did indeed come very, very close to making up for all of it!

11

A Startling Midnight Conversation

Mrs. Spilking had come around with Wolf for the bed check, and it was all Emily could do not to roll over, reach out a hand, and rub Wolf's ear when he came sniffing up to her cot. But she remained motionless on her side with her back to the door, her eyes tightly shut, and her hands safely under her coverlet. If Wolf's tail was wagging at an unusual rate, it was not noticed, just as Emily had hoped.

But after Mrs. Spilking left, she kept reviewing her conversation with Lucy and Sarah, and no matter how hard she tried, she could not drop off to sleep. The ponderous tolling of the hideous old clock in the Front Room, which could be heard in the rooms above it, first announced the hour of half past ten. Then eleven. Then half past eleven. And then, at last, twelve.

Emily now had to use the washroom. This was always an unpleasant thing to contemplate in a cold, dark room, but in the end, she reluctantly folded back her coverlet and dropped her feet onto the icy floor. Determining that she could make her way without a lantern, she tiptoed from the room in her bare feet so as not to waken Sarah and Lucy.

To her dismay, she found the washroom in use, for the door was tightly closed. And from behind the door came the sound of a girl sobbing bitterly! Emily's breath caught in her throat. The older girls had always appeared so composed, even though they were almost never seen to smile. She had thought they must be adjusted to the deadliness of Mrs. Spilking's Select Academy, but now she knew that they had simply taught their faces not to register their true feelings. Still, she could do nothing about it, and surely the girl would not wish to come out and find that someone had been standing outside the door listening.

Emily's first thought was that she should return to bed, forget her need for the washroom, and try to go to sleep. But then she looked through the door to that other washroom and had a bold thought. Why not use the princess's washroom?

There were no rules about it not being allowed when she was not using it, were there? Brave Emily ought not to be afraid to do something that did not require all that much bravery. But, in truth, brave Emily's heart was in her throat as she tiptoed toward the princess's royal washroom.

In the washroom, she was so intent on accomplishing her mission in the shortest possible time, she did not notice at first that she could hear voices coming from somewhere. As she listened, the voices grew louder. They were angry voices, and they were not just coming from "somewhere"; Emily now knew *exactly* where they were coming from . . . the room of Princess Delilla! She could even tell who owned the voices. One was that of the princess herself, and the other was that of . . . Mrs. Spilking!

And what Emily was hearing was most certainly an argument. Further, because no one was bothering to lower her voice, she could hear every word of it.

Eavesdropping, Emily believed, was no more acceptable now than it had been when she had overheard, through no fault of her own, the conversation between Mr. Crawstone and Mrs. Spilking weeks ago. Further, she was in even more danger now if she were discovered than she had been then. Quickly she started to leave the washroom. But with a hand already on the door handle, she suddenly dropped it. For she had heard something that made her determined to listen to more of the conversation. Oh, yes, very determined, indeed!

And so she remained in the washroom, still as a stone statue, listening. And it was not until the voices had lowered enough so that she believed the argument had abated, and Mrs. Spilking might soon be leaving the princess's room, that Emily scurried back to her own room. But by then she had heard everything she needed to know. Everything . . . and a great deal more!

The days had always passed slowly, but the day following Emily's bold excursion to "her royal majestry's" washroom seemed to drag by more slowly than ever. She was exploding with excitement and impatience to report what she had learned to Sarah and Lucy. She could hardly wait to see their faces when she told them.

The day finally came to an end. There was far too much to tell, however, in just the few minutes they had before they must climb into their beds. Therefore, Emily informed them they must positively try to stay awake and only feign sleep when Mrs. Spilking came around. Sarah and Lucy, of course, were so excited themselves, they could not have fallen asleep if their lives had depended on it. So at last they were all three seated cross-legged on a coverlet spread between Emily's and Sarah's cots. Emily had placed the oil lantern in the middle, and now its small flame fluttered on Sarah's and Lucy's eager faces.

"Well," began Emily, pausing to make the most of this thrilling moment, "it all began last night after you both were asleep, and I needed to use the washroom. When I arrived there, I found the washroom was already in use. The door was closed just as tight as it could be. But, oh, Lucy and Sarah, whoever was in there had not gone for the same reason I had. She was in there to cry! She was crying so hard, it quite broke my heart to hear her."

Emily's listeners, hanging on her every word, shook their heads in sympathy. "Did you find out who it was when she came out?" asked Sarah.

"Oh, I didn't wait until then," said Emily. "I didn't think whoever it was would like to know someone had been standing outside the door listening. So I didn't stay."

"Is—is that all that you wanted to tell us, Emily?" asked Lucy.

"Oh, no!" exclaimed Emily. She was hardly able to keep a cat-who-swallowed-a-mouse smile from her face. "That's only the beginning. There's lots, lots more. You see, I decided to use the princess's washroom!"

Sarah and Lucy gasped in delicious horror. "You *didn't*!" Sarah cried out.

"Yes, I did!" declared Emily. "And it was when I was in there that I heard voices. They came from Princess Delilla's room. One voice was hers, and the other belonged to Mrs. Spilking!"

Emily was again rewarded by horrified gasps. "Weren't you just terrified?" asked Lucy hopefully. "Did you fly back to your room then?"

"Oh, I would have," replied Emily. "And I was going to. But their voices were very loud, because they were having an argument. And I could hear every word they were saying."

"Do you mean Mrs. Spilking was actually having an argument with her pet?" asked Lucy, wide eyed with disbelief. "What was the argument about?"

"It . . . was . . . ," said Emily, drawing out the words as slowly as she could, "about . . . the . . . note!"

"The note?" Sarah repeated, gasping.

"Oh, yes, the note!" said Emily with a firm nod of her head. "And I shall tell you exactly what I heard Mrs. Spilking say. Well, not exactly, but as close as I can remember.

" 'You little fool!' is what she said. 'You stupid little fool!' "

Lucy's jaw fell. "Are you certain she was calling the princess *that*?"

"It's the person she was talking to," said Emily. "So of course it was the princess. But you mustn't interrupt, Lucy. Now I shall have to start from the beginning," she added pleasurably.

" 'You little fool! You stupid little fool! Did you think Mr. Binkwig was so blind he would not be paying attention to what was going on in the store even if he was waiting on another customer? Do you think he would not notice a young girl hand a note to the grocer's boy, who then gave her a sack of chocolates from the precious glass case without taking any money from her to bring to the counter?'

"Then the princess said, 'Well, he shouldn't have asked to see the note. It's unfair, and it's prying.'

"And Mrs. Spilking said, 'Unfair and prying, is it? If you are going to come up with excuses and reasons, you had better do better than that. It's his business, and he has every right to see such a note. And he was quite right to show it to me.'

"Then the princess said, 'I don't see how he even knew I wrote it. I was very careful not to sign my name.'

"This made Mrs. Spilking even more angry. 'You silly idiot! Mr. Binkwig was not born yesterday, my good girl. He has seen you and that grocer's boy of his making calf eyes at each other. He would have had no trouble figuring out who signed the letter "D," even if he had not been able to pry it out of the boy. Love notes to a grocer's boy! Oh, what folly! Stupid! Stupid! What could you have been thinking?' "

Emily paused to take a breath. "Well, as I said, that's not *exactly* what I heard them say. But it's close."

"A love note?" Lucy asked breathlessly.

Emily nodded. "Oh, yes! That's exactly what she had me carry in my pocket . . . a love note!"

"So the note never said anything about choco-lates at all?" asked Sarah.

"Well, it *had* to," replied Emily. "But it must have said other things as well."

"A love note!" Lucy repeated. "Oh!"

And then she and Sarah giggled nervously, for it was hard to know whether one should find this funny or shocking.

"Is—is the grocer's boy really handsome?" Sarah asked hesitantly. "He would have to be handsome, wouldn't he? I mean, think of all the handsome princes Princess Delilla has met."

Emily tilted her head, considering. "Yes, I believe he is. He is very handsome."

"What does he look like?" Lucy asked eagerly.

"Oh, he has very blue eyes and very dark wavy hair," replied Emily. "I should think he might pass for a prince."

"Well, I don't care how handsome he is," declared Lucy. "The princess shouldn't have let you be put in danger. I don't suppose *she'll* get put in the Cupboard for writing the note and then lying about it."

"Of course not!" replied Emily.

"But didn't Mrs. Spilking even say she might

tell you she's sorry she put you in the Cupboard by mistake?" asked Sarah.

"Not likely!" replied Emily with a toss of her head. "What she said was that a night in the Cupboard was a good lesson for a mealymouthed young girl, and all the other girls would profit from it, as well. So there you are!"

"Is that *everything* you heard?" Sarah asked, clearly hoping Emily's exciting report had not ended.

"Oh, no!" said Emily. "The very best part is still to come. Because guess what?"

"What?" asked both Sarah and Lucy breathlessly.

"Well," said Emily, "I now know who Princess Delilla is. And I know where she comes from. And I even know why she's here!"

12

A Very Suspicious Offer

The best part yet to come, Emily had announced. Elbows on their knees, Lucy and Sarah leaned forward, their glowing eyes riveted on Emily. Her midnight adventure had already provided enough thrills to make up for many dismal days past and many more to come. Now, unbelievably, there was yet another discovery to be reported, most amazingly the result of a simple trip to the washroom. It was almost too exciting to bear.

"Well," said Emily, "after Mrs. Spilking had finished with calling the princess stupid, she went on to say, 'To think of all the effort I have made to see that you might grow up a lady, and see how you repay me. A grocer's boy, Dolly! A grocer's boy!'"

"Dolly?" Sarah broke in. "Why was she calling the princess 'Dolly'?"

"Do you suppose it might be a short name for Delilla?" Lucy asked.

Emily smiled mysteriously. "Wait and see! I'm coming to that. Anyway, Mrs. Spilking went on, 'Look at all the things you're given here, everything you could possibly want. If you mind me, you might marry a rich man who can give you the same. Just what do you think a grocer's boy could provide for you, I ask you?'

"Then the princess said, 'Well, I love him. I do!'

"And Mrs. Spilking said, 'Pshaw! What do you know about love? You have a very good life here, with prospects. Yes, prospects, Dolly, my girl, and you had better be careful what you do.'

"And then the princess said, 'But it's so dull. Sometimes I think I will quite die from dullness, Ma.' "

With this, Emily stopped, waiting expectantly. She did not have to wait long.

"D-D-Did you say 'Ma'?" asked Lucy.

"That's exactly what I said!" replied Emily.

At this, both Sarah and Lucy threw their hands to their mouths, trying, albeit unsuccessfully, to repress squeals.

"Ma!" They both gasped.

"Yes!" Emily affirmed. "And she said it several

times, so I know I didn't make a mistake hearing it. Princess Delilla is no other than plain Dolly Spilking, and no more a princess than any of us. What do you think of that?"

The girls hardly needed to tell Emily what they thought of it, for the looks on their faces all but said it for them—looks of shock, surprise, disbelief, and total delight. Princess Delilla no more than plain Dolly Spilking! Who could ever have believed such a thing?

"Did they say more?" asked Lucy hopefully.

"Yes," replied Emily, "but I couldn't hear them very well after that, for they dropped their voices. I believed they had stopped arguing, and I was afraid Mrs. Spilking would come out at any moment, so I hurried back to our room."

"I don't suppose we can breathe a word to anyone about this either if we ever have the chance, can we?" asked Sarah.

"Oh, no!" cried Emily. "Not *anyone*! And we must never call her Dolly either, not even when we're alone. We might get into the habit of it and say it when we're in the washroom line or some place like that. We must go right on calling her Princess Delilla."

"Hmmmph!" Lucy said, sniffing. "It doesn't seem we have to worry about what to call her to her face. She never even *looks* at us. The stuck-up thing. She must really think she *is* a princess, but being called one doesn't make you one."

"Why, we could just call ourselves princesses, too, if we liked," said Sarah.

Emily thought a moment. "Yes, we could," she agreed. "When we're by ourselves, that's just what we could do. This can be *our* palace as much as hers and . . ." Emily began to get excited. "And we could have special names and—"

"And we could have royal meetings like this one," Sarah broke in.

"And think up adventures," added Lucy excitedly. "Mrs. Spilking could be the wicked stepmother queen and—and . . ." Lucy was too overcome to go on.

"But whatever we do, we have to be very, very careful that no one finds out. We can't be princesses anyplace but right here at night," Emily warned. And then, hearing the clock tolling the hour of twelve, she said, "But now we ought to get back to bed, or we'll fall face first into our porridge in the morning."

"Gruel provided by the wicked stepmother queen," Lucy corrected her.

"Yes, gruel," said Emily. "But does anyone have any ideas what they'd like to be called?"

It was remarkable how quickly the ideas arose. Instead of Emily Luccock, Sarah Tibbits, and Lucy Goodbody, who had climbed into bed the first time that night as three unhappy students of Mrs. Spilking's Select Academy for Young Ladies, it was now Princess Everbold, Princess Strongspirit, and Princess Lionheart, who climbed into bed for the second time as three happy princesses of their own private palace!

"The third meeting of the Palace Princesses will now come to order!" announced Princess Everbold, otherwise Emily Luccock.

It was after Mrs. Spilking and Wolf had made their nightly visit, and the three princesses were seated on the floor between Emily's and Sarah's cots again, the light from the flame of a fluttering lantern dancing in their eyes.

"Good thing Mrs. Crumble was dozing away again today," continued Princess Everbold. "I managed to hide the three strands of embroidery thread we each need. Did anyone else get any?"

The hands of the two other princesses instantly flew up.

"I got three pink ones," Princess Strongspirit, otherwise Sarah Tibbits, said eagerly.

"I got three yellow ones," said Princess Lionheart, otherwise Lucy Goodbody. "But you never did tell us what they're for. Do we get to know now?"

Princess Everbold grinned. "Well," she said, "they're for this!" She pulled from her pocket her three strands of embroidery thread, braided and knotted together to form a circle, which she set on her head. "There, you see, a crown! It was easy to make. I even made mine in the dark before Mrs. Spilking arrived."

"You *didn't!*" Princess Lionheart and Princess Strongspirit cried out, gasping.

"I did," said Princess Everbold. "But you can make yours now, and then we'll wear them at every meeting."

"Oh, Princess Everbold." Princess Lionheart sighed after she and Princess Strongspirit were wearing their crowns as well. "You *do* think of everything. You're the cleverest princess of us all!"

"No, I'm most surely *not!*" declared Princess Everbold. "Think of our last meeting, when we'd managed to get pencil stubs and folded pieces of drawing paper. The portraits Princess Strongspirit did of the wicked stepmother queen and her wicked stepdaughter looked exactly like Mrs. Spilking and Princess Delilla. You really are the best artist of all, Princess Strongspirit. And, Princess Lionheart, you're by far the best storyteller. I think we ought to go on right now with the story where the wicked stepmother queen and her wicked stepdaughter kidnap Princess Strongspirit."

"And then Princess Everbold and Princess Lionheart have to find a way to rescue her," said Princess Strongspirit. "I suppose they'll have to have the aid of a handsome prince, won't they?"

"A blindingly handsome prince," Princess Lionheart corrected her, "disguised as a grocer's boy with deep blue eyes and dark wavy hair."

"But *he's* the one yearned after by the wicked stepdaughter, isn't he?" asked Princess Strongspirit.

"Of course he is, silly," said Princess Lionheart. "But he's in love with only Princess Everbold, Princess Lionheart, and Princess Strongspirit."

Princess Strongspirit's eyes widened. "All *three* of them?"

"Well, maybe just one of them," replied Princess Lionheart after some consideration. "But don't forget, he probably has two blindingly handsome royal friends. I'm certain we can work something out, can't we, Princess Everbold? Is that too many complications?"

"Oh, no!" exclaimed Princess Everbold. "We need lots of complications!"

And they did. The more the better, for that was just something to look forward to at their meetings. And how much more wonderful all this was than looking forward to nothing but gray porridge, endless hoops of embroidery, dull books, and walks that passed for exercise, all repeated over and over again.

But Princess Everbold, as Emily, warned them over and over how the old people at Sugar Hill Hall had aroused suspicion when they began to look too cheerful and happy. So Emily, Sarah, and Lucy were very, very careful to go about during the day looking as downcast and dispirited as ever. They never exchanged telling glances over porridge or embroidery or during exercise or when they heard "terrifying" Wolf barking on the other side of the fence, and not even when they noted the looks of unbridled hatred Princess Delilla cast at Emily.

All the while, Emily had to fight to keep from her mind the fearful thought that she had yet to hear from Aunt and Uncle Twice. She kept telling herself that it must have taken a long time for them to reach India, and so it must take an equally long time for a letter to come in the opposite direction. But had not that long time come and gone? Was this not sure proof that she was indeed "not wanted"? How was she expected to forget about *that*?

She had by now, however, almost managed to forget about the ominous "all" until one afternoon, when she was coming into the dining room with the other girls after exercise in the yard, and Mrs. Crumble came up to her. After looking nervously over her shoulder toward the hall and Front Room doors, she put a hand on Emily's arm, stopping her before she could even hang up her coat on her wall peg.

"Please wait a moment, Emily," Mrs. Crumble said in a low, urgent voice. Then she added in a louder voice, "Girls, please return to your seats and begin your work. I shall be there in a moment."

Mrs. Crumble waited until every last girl had left the room before beginning to speak. What was it to be about? Emily's embroidery or knitting? She had never thought that Mrs. Crumble, so often dozing in her wing chair, ever paid a great deal of attention to the girls' work. Was Emily's so bad that she needed to be spoken to about it privately?

Mrs. Crumble dropped her voice again. "Emily, dear child, your aunt and uncle are in India, are they not?"

Totally unprepared for any question that was not to do with her embroidery or knitting, it took Emily a moment before she cautiously nodded. Cautiously, because, in truth, Mrs. Crumble continued to remind her so much of Mrs. Plumly . . . Mrs. Plumly, who had so deceived her at Sugar Hill Hall, feeding her little cakes and, in the end, tea that had something in it that caused Emily to reveal dangerous secrets. Embroidery and knitting? Oh, no. Mrs. Crumble must be leading up to something, and Emily intended to be very, very careful about what she said.

"Have you no relatives in New York, no friends you could go to if the need should ever arise?" asked Mrs. Crumble, an anxious frown creasing her pink cheeks.

Oh, if there were ever a trick question, this one was surely it! If Emily said "yes," then she might be asked to name them. And whom could she name? Mr. Crawstone, the only person she knew? Better to name a crocodile! So, no, she could not name a friend or relative, because she had none to name. There was nothing she could do but tell the truth. Even more cautiously now, she shook her head.

"Oh, my dear child, I was afraid of that!" said Mrs. Crumble, wringing her hands in anguish.

Actually wringing her hands . . . as good an actress as Mrs. Plumly! *Say nothing! Reveal nothing!* Emily warned herself.

"I had so hoped you would have a place to go if you should flee this place," Mrs. Crumble said sadly.

"Oh, but I don't wish to flee," promptly returned Emily, becoming as good an actress as Mrs. Crumble and Mrs. Plumly ever were. "I do love it so here!"

To that grand lie, Mrs. Crumble only shook her

head and sighed. "So frightened! Oh, so frightened!" she said under her breath. "Well, if anything should ever happen that you need a place to go, I want you to have this, child." With another quick, cautious look at both open doorways, she removed a bit of paper from her own pocket and slipped it into Emily's.

"Oh, I don't believe I shall ever need it," said Emily earnestly. "But I do thank you so much. I do, indeed."

Emily did not need to look at the bit of paper to know that it contained the address of Mrs. Crumble's home. What she had told Mrs. Crumble was the absolute truth, that she would never need it. For even if she ever had to do such a dangerous thing as fleeing the school, she would as soon have run to Mrs. Crumble's home as named Mr. Crawstone as a friend! But what was behind all this in the first place? Finally, Emily came up with the answer.

Mrs. Spilking wished to know if Emily could be as easily persuaded by Mrs. Crumble to do something as she had been by Princess Delilla! Would not that be another fine excuse to send Emily back to the Cupboard as a further example to the other girls? Well, Mrs. Spilking had better try something else. Emily had been hoodwinked by Princess Delilla. She would not be hoodwinked by Mrs. Crumble!

Satisfied that that was the answer to Mrs. Crumble's mysterious behavior, Emily was able finally to put it from her mind. All she knew was that she must be very careful about such tricks being played on her. Further, Mrs. Crumble was to be trusted as little as Mrs. Spilking.

That night, Lucy and Sarah were greatly inclined to agree with Emily's appraisal of the situation. They were, of course, dreadfully disappointed that Mrs. Crumble, fearful though she was of Mrs. Spilking, could be persuaded by her to do something so wicked. And while they had always doubted Emily's comparison of her to the hideously evil Mrs. Plumly of Sugar Hill Hall, they were beginning to believe that Emily might just be right.

It was not until much later that night, however, as Emily lay staring into the dark, once again unable to drop off to sleep, that she began thinking. And thinking. And wondering. And then suddenly, she shivered. It was not from the cold, but from suddenly beginning to consider that she might have been entirely wrong about the reasons for Mrs. Crumble's offer of her home in case Emily should ever need it. Oh, not that Emily trusted Mrs. Crumble. Not one bit. But what if . . . what if, in some frightening way, this actually had something to with "all"!

13

Doomed!

A week passed by, and nothing further happened to make Emily believe one thing or another about Mrs. Crumble's "kind offer" of her home should Emily need it. Then one morning, when letters had been written and passed to Mrs. Spilking for inspection, she flared her eyes in Emily's direction. "Before going to the Front Room, Emily, you will please meet with me in my office. That will be all, the rest of you."

A private conversation with Mrs. Crumble now being followed by a private conversation with Mrs. Spilking! Lucy and Sarah cast anxious glances at Emily as she followed Mrs. Spilking from the dining room.

In her office, Mrs. Spilking pointed a sharp finger at one of the two stiff, unwelcoming wooden chairs that stood at attention before her desk. "You may sit, if you wish," she said. And while Emily perched timidly on the edge of one of the chairs, hands folded, Mrs. Spilking pulled open a drawer and lifted out two envelopes.

"I have two letters here," she said, her long, bony fingers toying with them. "One is actually addressed to me, but I wish you to read it. The second, which you may read first, I believe is from your aunt and uncle in India."

A letter from Aunt and Uncle Twice at long last! Emily eagerly reached for it, barely noticing the calculating look given her by Mrs. Spilking when she handed it over. Nor did Emily care that the envelope opened so easily there was not much doubt it had been opened earlier. Never mind, it was a letter, the longed-for letter! But Emily's heart was not nearly so light when she finished reading it as when she had begun. For this is what she read in the letter written by Aunt Twice:

> *Dear, darling Emily,*
>   *What was our delight in finding a letter from you waiting for us when we arrived in India, along with a letter of welcome from Mr. Slyde! Our ship had experienced serious difficulties and delayed us*

to such a degree that the ship bearing your letter actually arrived before we did. And now a second letter from you has also arrived. But the best part is that you love your school so much. Uncle Twice and I cannot tell you how happy that makes us!

There are unfortunately many things that have to be seen to, so many arrangements made, which is why this letter is so short. And, sadly, it may be a very long time before you hear from us again.

Now I must go. I pray that, for your sake and ours, you will continue happily in your school. And try always to be a brave girl, no matter what!

Your loving Aunt Twice and Uncle Twice

Here was the letter Emily had awaited for such a very long time, a letter that should have set her heart dancing. Why was it that it filled her with such foreboding? "Be a brave girl, no matter what!" Why those ominous words once more? And why must it be such a long time before Emily would hear from Aunt and Uncle Twice again? All Emily could think was that Baby Cousin Twice was to take up so much of their time, there would be none left for writing to *her*. And they did not have to suffer a shred of guilt because, after all, was not Emily reporting in her letters that she was as happy as she could be in school?

Well, Aunt Twice was certainly true to her word. For the date on the letter revealed it *had* been a long time since it was written. If Aunt or Uncle Twice had written every week, as Emily did, several letters should have arrived by now, not just one. Emily had to fight to hold back tears, for to weep in front of Mrs. Spilking was unthinkable.

"I trust your aunt and uncle are well?" she asked.

Emily dutifully nodded, knowing full well that Mrs. Spilking had already read the letter.

"You may, of course, keep that letter," she said. "But now I wish you to read this one, the one written to me." She handed the letter to Emily, pretending to be busy with papers on the desk, but looking at her the whole time from under lowered eyelids. The letterhead announced that it was from "SCREWITCH, CHIZZLE & SLYDE—Attorneys at Law," addressed to Mrs. Felonius Spilking of Mrs. Spilking's Select Academy for Young Ladies. And this is the letter Emily read:

> *My very dear Madam:*
> *It is with the deepest regret that I must write this letter to you regarding one of the young girls who is a present student and boarder at your most*

highly regarded academy. That girl is Miss Emily Luccock. I must tell you that a most excellent friend of mine, Mr. Ichabod Crawstone, to whom your fine academy was unreservedly recommended, in turn recommended it to Miss Luccock's aunt and uncle, Mr. and Mrs. William Luccock, via myself.

You, of course, were apprised from the outset that all money due you on Miss Luccock's behalf would come from me. I believe I have to this date been faithful in fulfilling that obligation.

Perhaps you should know that it was only the most unfortunate of circumstances that led to Mr. Luccock's decision to remove to India with Mrs. Luccock, a decision that entailed the sad necessity of leaving their niece behind in this country.

Unable, however, to provide the means to place his niece in your highly esteemed academy, he regretfully agreed to allow her *fortune to be used for this purpose. After making certain investments on her behalf, he honored me by placing that fortune, in its entirety, in my trust.*

Now a calamitous event has occurred, the catastrophic sudden failure of all the investments Mr. Luccock made on behalf of his niece. It is with the deepest regret, my very good madam, that I must tell you Miss Emily Luccock is now penniless. She is no longer an heiress. Her entire fortune is, alas, lost.

As Mr. Luccock is totally unable to support her at your most valued academy, I must ask that you temper with mercy any action you may deem necessary to take in regard to this young girl, and ask that she not be simply put out, for she has no place to go. Recognizing that you do not operate a charitable institution, and need income for your most superior academy to remain in business, might I ask that you perhaps find something for Miss Luccock to do there to assist you in some way?

I have already written a letter to Mr. and Mrs. Luccock, a letter that went out in the very same mail as this one. Unfortunately, as you know, a reply as to their intentions will take some time in reaching me. I must beg your indulgence in this. If you have further questions about this most unfortunate situation, please do not hesitate to write me.

In the meantime, my very, very dear madam, we must throw ourselves on your mercy.

> *With the utmost regard, I remain*
> *Your respectful servant,*
> *Josiah Slyde*

Emily, a pauper! Thrown on the mercy of Mrs. Spilking! And for how long was that to be? The two months or so it might take to hear from Uncle Twice? And hear what? That Emily was to be immediately placed on a ship and sent to India? To an aunt and uncle who were too occupied with their present affairs even to write her more than one, pitifully short note? That is to say, provided they even had the money to pay her passage, which it appeared they did not.

Emily had made up her mind that she might be at Mrs. Spilking's Select Academy for a very long time. But the "very long time" had had a number attached to it, five and one half years, at which time she would come into her fortune. Now, suddenly, she was no longer an heiress. There was no fortune. She was penniless! The question was what was to become of her now, being thrown upon the mercy of Mrs. Spilking?

Mrs. Spilking was in no hurry to make her pronouncement. Keeping Emily in agonizing suspense, she retrieved the letter, very, very carefully folded it up, slid it back into the envelope, and laid it on the desk before her in Emily's full view. Then she placed her elbows on her desk, rested her sharp chin on her knuckles, and flared her eyes at Emily.

"Well, and what *are* we to do with you?" she asked with a coy little smile, as if what Emily thought made the slightest bit of difference.

Emily could only shrug. What else was there to do?

"Now, as you read in Mr. Slyde's letter, Emily, this is not a charitable institution," said Mrs. Spilking. "While the families of each girl do pay us, each girl also costs us a great deal of money."

As Mrs. Spilking paused for Emily to digest this financial revelation, Emily thought of the gray porridge, stale bread, and potato and turnip stew, the dog-eared books, and the pencil stubs that cost Mrs. Spilking such "a great deal of money" and could not help but suspect that a much *greater* deal of money from the girls' tuitions was reserved for Mrs. Spilking herself, and particularly for the luxuries enjoyed by her daughter, Dolly.

"So," continued Mrs. Spilking, satisfied that enough of what she had said had sunk into Emily, "you can understand why I cannot keep a girl here for charitable reasons. However, as Mr. Slyde has written such an eloquent appeal on your behalf, I shall give no thought to sending you to some institution where girls with no visible means of support are placed. No, I shall allow you to remain here, certainly until Mr. Slyde has received some word from your uncle in India." Mrs. Spilking paused to flare her eyes again at Emily.

"Th-Th-Thank you, Mrs. Spilking," mumbled Emily, recognizing that an expression of gratitude was expected of her.

"But . . . ," said Mrs. Spilking with another warning flare, "as Mr. Slyde suggested that I might find something for you to do here, to earn your keep, as it were, I shall do just that. Since I have no need for an assistant, as Mr. Slyde has mentioned, you will be allowed to remain here as a servant, Emily, but no longer as a student. You will, therefore, no longer be permitted to attend classes. You will, however, remain in your room upstairs until I can make arrangements for a cellar room, all of which are in use at the moment. In fact, you may remain upstairs until a new student comes to take your place or until something is heard from your uncle, whichever comes first. But never forget, not for one moment, that you are now a servant. Is that understood?"

How could it not be understood? Nothing could have been clearer. And while Emily was to be allowed the privilege of remaining in the room with Lucy and Sarah, she was always to have the fear of being removed. Oh, yes, it was understood! Emily Luccock was once again to be a servant with a future that included living in a cellar. It was as if nothing had changed. Nothing!

Understood? Yes, indeed, it was understood! Slowly, Emily nodded.

14

Bella Speaks Out

Lucy and Sarah, as was to be expected, were shocked and horrified by the new development.

"Oh, Emily!" cried Sarah. "A servant at Mrs. Spilking's dreadful Select Academy!"

"It's bad enough to be a student here!" exclaimed Lucy.

"And—and we won't be able to be princesses anymore," said Sarah, tears in her eyes.

"Whyever not?" asked Emily, who, as it turned out, found herself having to cheer up a totally downcast Lucy and Sarah, instead of the other way around.

"How can we be?" asked Lucy. "You'll be in the cellar, where Bella lives, and we'll be up here. How will we be able to have our royal meetings?"

"Well, we *will* be able to," declared Emily,

attempting a smile, "because I haven't told you the good part."

"You mean there's actually a good part?" asked Sarah.

"There actually is," replied Emily. "Mrs. Spilking says there's no room to put me in the cellar, so I'll get to stay right here!"

"Oh, Emily!" exclaimed Lucy and Sarah, breaking into smiles.

"Of course," Emily hurried to say, "it might not be forever. It depends on what Uncle Twice writes back after he has heard from Mr. Slyde. And if Mrs. Spilking gets a new student for this room, I'll have to move out. Then, I suppose, she'll have to find a place for me in the cellar. But for now, we can go on having our royal meetings right here!"

"Then let's hope the old stepmother witch never gets another student!" said Sarah.

"We'll hang a sign in front telling everyone who comes that this is a horrid place and that they shouldn't apply!" added Lucy.

"Do you suppose what Mrs. Crumble said to you had anything to do with this?" Sarah asked.

"Sarah, it couldn't have," Lucy said. "That happened days ago, and the letter just came. Perhaps

Mrs. Crumble was really trying to be helpful."

But to this, Emily could only shake her head. "I saw the date on the letter. It must have come days before Mrs. Crumble talked to me about fleeing. I think it was Mrs. Spilking's idea, hoping I might try to run away. If she caught me and then told me about being a pauper, she would have a good excuse to put me in a . . . in a home for wayward girls—or even a workhouse."

"A home for wayward girls or a workhouse!" Lucy repeated, gasping.

"You're probably right, Emily," said Sarah indignantly. "But now look, she's got herself a nice free servant!"

"Well, she *does* have to pay for my food," said Emily.

Upon hearing this, Lucy and Sarah looked at her with disbelief. "Then don't eat too much porridge," said Lucy. "You really are quite amazing, Emily. You're so . . . brave."

"I've been a servant before, and I lived to tell about it," said Emily. "Remember?"

"I don't care, Emily. You *are* brave," said Lucy. "I'd be in a puddle if it happened to me!"

But the truth was that Emily *was* in a puddle.

She had to fight back tears that night, the last night before she began her role as a servant girl. She had been a servant when she first came to Sugar Hill Hall, with very little hope that she would ever be anything else. But somehow, this was different. She had endured so much before, but she had finally begun a wonderful new life with Aunt and Uncle Twice. She was even returned to being an heiress again, one day to be possessed of an enormous fortune.

Now all that had been snatched away with the arrival of two letters. She had been lightly dismissed by Aunt and Uncle Twice by the "many things that have to be seen to," and the little over five years until she would come into her fortune had been turned into never!

If only she could stop thinking of both these things, especially when she lay in bed each night, she might not have minded quite so much her new life at Mrs. Spilking's Select Academy. At least she no longer had to develop a stiff neck from bending over embroidery hoops, poke her eyes out knitting in the near darkness, read unbelievably dull books, or march 'round and 'round the dismal yard. But when she tried to persuade Sarah and Lucy of the one or two benefits provided by her new role as servant, purely in order to raise their spirits, she had very little success. They simply could not see anything beneficial about it.

Then one night, as they sat on the floor holding their meeting of the Palace Princesses by the light of the lantern, Emily suddenly had an idea. Scrambling to her feet, she went to her dress hanging on its wall peg and drew a key from the pocket. Then, asking a puzzled Lucy and Sarah if she could borrow the lantern for a few minutes, promising to return with a surprise, she left them in darkness as she tiptoed from the room and down the stairs. No, not the front stairs, which as a student she was required to use, but the stairs Bella used, which did not pass right by Mrs. Spilking's parlor. Well, as a servant like Bella, was it not perfectly proper that Emily should use those stairs as well?

The only light in the hall at the foot of the stairs came from the lantern Emily held, for not a single lamp fluttered on the wall. Mrs. Spilking had turned them all off for the night. And as Emily crept through the dining room and looked through the hall doorway, she could see that there was not even a sliver of light coming from Mrs. Spilking's parlor. Once in the kitchen, key in hand, she made for a cupboard on the back wall. But then she came to a sudden stop, her heart pounding. Through the deep silence, she had heard the sound of footsteps!

Swiftly, Emily dove under the kitchen table against the wall, turned off her lantern, and pushed herself back as far as she could, drawing her knees up under her chin. Afraid even to breathe, she waited, as the footsteps drew nearer and nearer. Then they came right through the kitchen door, accompanied by the dim flicker of lantern light. Holding the lantern and wearing a gray flannel robe and outrageously bright pink beaded slippers was Mrs. Spilking!

Yawning hugely, she headed straight for the very same cupboard that had been Emily's destination. With a key drawn from her robe pocket, she unlocked the cupboard and took from it a round tin box with a small china plate sitting on top. Then she carried the box and plate, along with the lantern, and set them right down on the table under which Emily was cowering. *Plunk! Plunk!* She could hear them come down right over her head. Then there was the *plunk* of the plate coming down from the tin. This was followed by the sound of metal scraping against metal, accompanied by a grunt from Mrs. Spilking as she labored to pry the lid off the tin. Then she began to mutter to herself, clearly counting something.

"One, two, three, um, um, um. Well, they're all still here. Bella hasn't been helping herself. Now, let's see, which ones to choose, um, um, um. I believe I'll have two."

This conversation with herself successfully completed, Mrs. Spilking replaced the lid on the tin and returned it to the cupboard, which she carefully locked. Then she retrieved the plate left sitting on the table and, finally, with another shuddering yawn, left the kitchen.

Even after the *flap-flapping* of Mrs. Spilking's pink beaded slippers had faded, Emily remained under the table, too frozen to move. What if Mrs. Spilking had brought Wolf along, wagging his tail and sniffing under the table, as he would most assuredly have done? That would have been the instant end of Emily. Off to the school for wayward girls for *her*! And would Mrs. Spilking not have had an excellent excuse now to send her there? Skulking around the kitchen late at night, prepared to steal. Yes, to *steal*! For was not the key in her nightdress pocket intended for the very cupboard where Mrs. Spilking kept locked the treats reserved for herself and her precious Princess Delilla?

And where, pray tell, had that key come from? In truth, it was from Bella, who had found an extra key and given it to Emily. But Emily would have allowed herself to be sent off to join the wayward girls rather than disclose this to Mrs. Spilking. For when Bella had given Emily the key, she had said it was for no particular reason, "just be certain that whatever disappears from the cupboard"—wink, wink—"is not something Mrs. Spilking can easily count."

Well, this was not something Emily needed to think about now, because neither she nor the key in her pocket had been discovered under the kitchen table. But after she had taken a few minutes to begin breathing properly again, her first thought was that she had better forget her grand plans and fly back to her room. Her second thought was the same. But by the time she had arrived at her third thought, she had entirely changed her mind. Mrs. Spilking would surely not return that night, and Lucy and Sarah were

upstairs waiting patiently in the dark for a big surprise. And had Emily's whole plan not been to
impress on them that being a servant had its benefits? What kind of benefit was it that she had had a
terrifying near encounter with Mrs. Spilking, and
risked a possible one-way trip to the home for
wayward girls? No, Emily decided at last, she must
complete the mission.

Of course, having had to turn off her lantern, she
was now in total darkness. But she did know the
shelf on which Mrs. Slump kept the matches for
lighting the stove. Cautiously feeling her way over
to it, she soon had the lantern lit again and once
more approached the locked cupboard. Her hand
was shaking as she fitted the key into the lock. This,
after all, was where Mrs. Spilking had been, doing
the very same thing only minutes before.

The cupboard door open, she found herself
looking at the very same tin that Mrs. Spilking had
just held in her hands. That one Emily would not
touch for her life, for she was certain it contained
the little frosted cakes, counted "one, two, three,
um, um, um" by Mrs. Spilking. There were other
tins and boxes as well, but in the end, Emily took
only some dry "bisks" from the basket heaped

with them. Just as Bella had said that first night when she had brought some to Emily, no one would miss them. Still, Emily was careful to take only three to put in her nightdress pocket, one for Lucy, one for Sarah, and one for herself.

Smart, brave Emily! On her way back to their room, fearing every second that Mrs. Spilking might just put in another appearance, Emily considered having "smart" win out over "brave" and never trying this again. But she knew that when she saw how excited Lucy and Sarah would be over this late-night royal feast, she might very well decide to reverse the "smart" "brave" order, and perhaps "brave" would win out!

Lucy and Sarah, as it turned out, were not nearly so thrilled with Emily's "royal feast" as she had thought they would be. After all, it *was* only plain, very dry biscuits, one each. They were both terribly polite, of course, and did say "thank you" over and over. But when Emily told them about the encounter with Mrs. Spilking, Lucy actually used the word "stupid" when referring to the risk taken by Emily.

As for ownership of the key changing anyone's opinion of her becoming a servant at Mrs.

Spilking's Select Academy, Sarah only allowed weakly that it *might* improve upon it a bit. Lucy said flatly it did no such thing, and the sooner someone discovered a terrible mistake had been made, and returned Emily to her proper place in the school, the better. So "smart" finally won out over "brave" after all!

Bella, on the other hand, although just as certain that Emily was "done wrong" by someone, was far more interested in the fact that Emily had so readily taken to her servant's role. Bella, in truth, never ceased to be astonished by it, and she told Emily so on every possible occasion.

"I ain't ever!" she declared once more as she and Emily stood at the sink one evening "doing up" the end results of Mrs. Slump's dinner preparations after she had gone. "Washing, ironing, dusting, scraping pots and pans. You're a wonder is all I can say." Bella paused to shake her head. "Ain't ever seen the like! Now, tell me more 'bout Tilly what you said taught you all you know. Was she really as mean as all that?"

Emily, of course, had by now had plenty of time to tell Bella about the early horrors of Sugar Hill

Hall, and Bella never tired of asking more questions about it, Tilly being of special interest because she was a servant just as Bella was.

"Oh, she was dreadfully mean, Bella," replied Emily, busy polishing a dish. "But, as I said, she turned out to be kindhearted as she could be, and we ended up the best of friends."

"Was that Mrs. Meeching 'bout the same as Madam?" asked Bella.

"Probably close to the same," said Emily.

"I ain't surprised," said Bella grimly. "But hard for me believing anyone's so wicked as Madam here is. Keeping that dog just to scare the wits out o' the girls. That dog scare you, Emily?" While seemingly giving all her attention to scraping something off the sink, Bella gave Emily a sideways look.

Emily, herself suddenly intent on polishing another dish, mumbled something and then quickly darted a sideways look at Bella as well.

Back and forth went the sideways looks, until at last Bella could contain herself no longer. "You know, don't you?"

Emily bit her lip and nodded.

"How'd you find out?" asked Bella. "You ain't

ever been 'round that dog excepting maybe once when you first come here."

"He pushed the Cupboard door open when I was in there being punished," said Emily. "I just knew he was going to rip me to shreds, but instead he came up and licked my chin. He's gentle as a kitten, Bella! I—I just don't understand why he growled at me when I first arrived here."

"Hmmmph!" Bella snorted. "'Twasn't you, Emily. 'Twas that flippin' Mr. Crawstone. Dog growls its head off every time that man gets too close when he comes visiting Madam S. *He's* the one most likely to get ripped to shreds one day, if you wish my opinion. Anyways, you know the secret 'bout Wolf, and now you got your answer 'bout the growling."

Bella hesitated, then looked sideways at Emily again. "Would you like to know another secret?"

Emily quickly nodded.

"All right, then," said Bella. "The secret is that Wolf ain't a he at all. Wolf's a she, and Wolf ain't even her name. It's Willa!"

"Willa!" Emily exclaimed.

"That's right!" said Bella. "A real jewel she is, and belonging to someone who don't even like dogs. Just kept for the purpose o' scaring everyone. She's left outside in that flippin' yard with that old dog-house o' hers most o' the time or else tied up in the cellar. But I see she gets her walk most nights, poor thing. Mrs. Spilking lets me take her out after you're all gone to bed. I feel real scared going 'bout nights most times, but never when I'm with Willa."

"Does Mrs. Spilking know that you know?" asked Emily.

Bella shrugged. "It ain't anything we have discussions 'bout. She slipped once and said Willa 'stead o' Wolf, which is why I know her name. But 'round Madam, I just keep pretending I don't know a boy dog from a girl dog, and go on calling her Wolf."

Bella now paused to deliver yet another sideways glance in Emily's direction. "You in on any other house secrets?"

Emily started, very nearly dropping the cup she was polishing. Then she again mumbled something that could have passed for "yes" or "no," and did not look Bella in the eye. But Bella had no intention of letting this pass.

"Well, which is it?" she demanded to know.

"I . . . I guess it's 'yes,'" replied Emily faintly.

"All right," said Bella. "This place got two secrets. You already found out 'bout one. How'd you find out 'bout the other? I mean, it's her majestry we're talking 'bout, ain't it?"

Emily nodded. "I—I heard an argument she had with Mrs. Spilking when I went to use her bathroom late one night. She—she called Mrs. Spilking 'Ma.'"

To this, Bella shook her head and sighed. "Took me three years 'fore I found out. You ain't been here but a few months and already know it all. And good at keeping secrets, too. Too bad you ain't going to be in service permanent. But you ain't, Emily. I got a serious feeling in my bones that you ain't!"

15

An Unexpected Visitor

Well, Bella's bones might be telling her that Emily's days as a servant were numbered, but as more days went by with nothing changing, Emily concluded that she must make up her mind this was to be her life forever.

It had been a shock at first, especially waiting on the girls at mealtimes instead of sitting down with them. And she had to endure the looks of triumph Princess Delilla gave her at every opportunity. Once she even nudged Emily's arm deliberately when she was trying to pour some watered-down tea into a cup on the table. The tea naturally sloshed all over the girl sitting next to Princess Delilla, and Emily had to endure a grand lecture on clumsiness from Mrs. Spilking. But now she was getting used to waiting on table and had learned how to avoid Princess Delilla's elbow when passing near her.

Emily knew, however, she would rather return to being a student in a minute, even if it meant suffering through endless hoops of embroidery, dull, ragged books, and deadly "exercise" periods. Perhaps it was only because she once had hope for her future as a student, whereas now there was none. All she had left to count on was the feeling in Bella's bones. In the meantime, she must try to keep up her spirits, reminding herself how fortunate she was to have such staunch supporters and friends as Bella, Lucy, and Sarah.

But Emily did not feel quite so fortunate about her now-closer acquaintance with Mrs. Slump. She was so very large and violent, and the kitchen so very small, that when she began banging pots and pans around, as was her usual manner of preparing food, Emily often feared serious injury if she were in the kitchen at the same time. Still, her job included helping Mrs. Slump, so help her she must.

Mrs. Slump being as large as she was, and the cellar stairs being as narrow as they were, one of Emily's chores was to go down to the cellar and fetch the potatoes, the turnips, the lard, and the dry cereal. The latter, of course, then required that Emily pick out the weevils. This job was once done by Mrs. Slump herself, if she even thought about it before preparing the porridge. Otherwise, she would boil the porridge, weevils and all. But Emily never minded the trips to the cellar to fetch supplies for Mrs. Slump or, for that matter, to help Bella with the washing and ironing, which took place down there. At least she did not mind them as much as she thought she would. But she would not want to *live* in the cellar. Never again! Not then ... not *ever*!

Another task Emily performed for Mrs. Slump was peeling. Mrs. Slump hated peeling. If it were up to her, the potatoes and turnips would undoubtedly be hurled into the stew in their original state.

"Peeling comes close to goormette cooking. If Madam wishes my goormette cooking, she pays for goormette cooking," Mrs. Slump announced to Emily, slamming a pot on the stove. So while Emily peeled or picked weevils from the cereal, Mrs. Slump lowered herself into a chair at the kitchen table and sipped tea from her favorite cracked green china cup while regaling Emily with stories of her life. In truth, Emily came to enjoy these more peaceful moments with Mrs. Slump, who could be jolly and entertaining when she was not rampaging around the kitchen.

But when Mrs. Slump was at the height of her cooking fervor, Emily stayed out of her way and came into the kitchen only when all was quiet. Which is what she did one day to fetch a cup of water before Mrs. Slump was due to arrive to prepare the stew for dinner. When Emily entered the kitchen, however, she found somebody already there.

It was a boy about her age, standing at the sink, intent on the job of cleaning a large fish. He was attacking the task with such energy that fish scales were flying all over the counter. Some even seemed to be flying into his red curls and the green scarf he had wound around his neck.

Bright red curls, brighter even than Lucy's, and a familiar green scarf! Emily threw a hand to her mouth to repress a shriek. "Kipper!"

The boy turned around, saw Emily, and produced a wide grin. But while he most definitely did have red curls, blue eyes brighter than the sea, and ruddy cheeks, he just as definitely was *not* Kipper.

"Wrong boy," he said cheerfully. "But close 'nough. Kipper's my cuz."

"P–P–Piper?" stammered Emily.

"The very one!" replied the boy, wiping his nose with the back of his hand, paying no attention to the fish scales decorating it. "You must be Miss Emily."

Emily could do no more than nod, for her brain was still spinning. Piper, her friend Kipper's cousin, actually standing right before her!

"I never thought as how I'd find you here so easy," said Piper. "I decided if I arrived at the front door o' this place asking for you, they'd just slam it in my face. So I figgered I'd come to the servants' entry, *not* asking for you, but selling fish from my pa's shop. There's more than one way to trap a tuna, as Pa always says.

"But wasn't so easy getting in that way, neither. Appears like the owner ain't willing to spend two cents more'n she has to feeding the inmates, and the cook ain't willing to clean a fish. Too much like peeling, and smelly besides. Leastways that's what someone named Bella, who answered the bell when I rung it, said."

"So how *did* you ever manage to get in here?" asked Emily.

"Well, this Bella told me that I had to practically offer the owner, name of Mrs. Spilking, a fish for just 'bout nothing and then offer myself to clean it. So I offered one, and then I offered th' other, and here I am. Didn't have a idea how I was to see you, howsumever, you being a student, like Kipper's pa wrote. Then here you go and show up slick as a sardine what found its way through a hole in the net, as Pa always says. But why are you out here in a apron what looks like you been housecleaning? Ain't you supposed to be studying your lessons?"

Emily bit her lip, hesitating. "I—I'm not a student anymore. I've become a servant again, the way I was when I first met Kipper."

"Wheeoo!" Piper whistled. "How come, Miss Emily? What happened?"

"Oh, you mustn't call me Miss Emily," she said quickly. "Kipper never did, and you mustn't, either. But what happened is that my Aunt and Uncle Twice went to India, and—and didn't take me with them because I don't believe they wish me to live with them anymore. Then the fortune I had, which was to pay for my school was all lost. Someone has written to my uncle about it, but I don't believe that will change anything. So there you are. It—it's really very simple."

"Don't sound simple to me," said Piper. "And I know Kipper won't like it when he hears. He ain't much o' a hand at writing, but his pa, who's my Uncle Ab, wrote my pa, so I know Kipper was pleased as the mackerel who swallowed the minnow, as my pa always says, when your uncle got found, and you got to be a hairess. Now, quicker 'n any wink, your uncle's gone again, taking your aunt with him, and you ain't got a penny left. You know, something don't sound right to me 'bout it. Can't help thinking what I come to tell you 'bout's got something to do with it."

"I was wondering why you had come looking for me," Emily said. "Kipper gave me a note telling me about you, but I never thought I'd ever see you, even when I was still a student here. Mrs. Spilking keeps all the girls practically prisoners. This isn't a very nice place, Piper. But what is it you came to tell me?"

"Might be something, and might be nothing," said Piper, thoughtfully pulling on an ear, his fingers leaving a few fish scales in their wake. "But seems as how Kipper went back to that big old mansion he says got the name o' Sugar Hill Hall.

He wanted to see if whoever bought it from your uncle might want to be reg'lar customers buying his pa's fish. But when he got there, he rung the bell at the back, and then he banged on the door. But nobody came to answer. Then he got brave and went out front and did the same. Still nobody came. He figgered as how everybody was out, but seemed pecoolyar—a big place like that ain't got a servant to come to the door. Anyway, back home Kipper went."

"Perhaps if the owners were away," said Emily, "the servants were just taking naps or something."

"You mean taking a few winks on the sly?" said Piper. "Might o' crossed Kipper's mind, 'cause he decided as how he'd give it 'nother try. So back he went, ringing and banging, banging and ringing. Then, getting to wondering, he went and hoisted himself up to look in a window. Then he looked in more windows. And guess what, Emily?"

"I couldn't," replied Emily.

"Nothing in the house!" said Piper. "No people, no furnishings . . . not a blamed thing but dust lying all over. Ain't anybody living there, Emily, and that's the truth! Thinking something ain't right, and wondering if it got anything to do with you, Kipper had Uncle Ab write my pa and asked him to try to find you to tell you 'bout it. Lucky you told Kipper the name o' this school. Pa dug 'round and 'round, and somehow or other found out where it was. But you got to wonder as how Kipper, who ain't got any notion o' your present situation, got it in his head 'bout something not being right with that old house sitting there all dark and dusty and empty as a shell with the crab missing, as Pa always says, and thinking as how it got a connection to you. Now, that's mighty pecoolyar, ain't it?"

"It really is, Piper," said Emily. "But I don't know what connection there could be. My Uncle Twice sold Sugar Hill Hall, and he and Aunt Twice are already in India. Mrs. Meeching and Mrs. Plumly, who used to be there, are now in jail for all their wrongdoings. My fortune got lost because . . . because Uncle Twice didn't manage it very well. So now I've become a servant. I can't see how nobody living in Sugar Hill Hall could have much to do with all that."

"Maybe not," said Piper uncertainly. "But now that I know how to find you, I'll let you know if we hear more 'bout it from Uncle Ab. And if you ever need anything, here on this bit o' paper is where Pa's fish shop is. Pa and me live over it. It's a pretty long ways away. Had to take a bunch o' trolleys to get here. But good for you to know 'bout it anyways. Sorry 'bout the paper being all crumpled and smelling so powerful of fish. Oops! Sounds like someone's coming. Never mind, I'm 'bout done, anyways."

Someone was indeed coming, and moments later Mrs. Slump thumped into the kitchen. She eyed Piper suspiciously as she hung up her coat and removed a great, squashed red hat from her head.

"I'm Mrs. Slump, the cook," she said sourly. "And who might you be?"

"I'm Piper," he said. "You got bought some nice mackerel, fresh as you please. And I'm cleaning it for you. Comes with the price, you might say."

"Now, ain't that nice!" said Mrs. Slump, rewarding Piper with an expansive beam. "Cleaning it and all. Good thing, or it might o' gone into the dump. Don't like cleaning. Don't like peeling. Might just cook up a goormette dinner tonight. You can run along now, fish boy. Emily will let you out. Emily, you hurry back. We got work to do!"

Mrs. Slump was already slamming a pot on the stove as Emily led Piper out of the kitchen, down the cellar steps, and on to the stairwell leading to the street. She hated to see him leave, for who knew how long it would be before she would see him again. But Piper promised he would be back even if there was no further news from Kipper. Then with a smile and a wave, he was gone, and Emily had to fly back to the kitchen to help Mrs. Slump with her "goormette" meal.

And, oh, what a grand introduction Mrs. Spilking gave the dinner that evening. A very, very special treat, she informed the girls, and she but hoped they would appreciate what it had cost her to provide this outstandingly fresh fish from the sea. One might have thought Mrs. Spilking had rowed into the ocean herself to catch the fish—a fish that might well have been a charitable donation from Piper's pa's fish shop for all it cost her, a fish cleaned by Piper so Mrs. Slump would then deign to cut it up for the potato-turnip stew, and finally, a fish that would not have been there at all but for Emily, who had the great pleasure of serving it to Mrs. Spilking and Princess Delilla before she could even taste it later in the kitchen with Bella.

But Emily hardly minded, for she had now actually met Kipper's cousin! And while he did not have *exactly* the same bright red curls or blue eyes or ruddy cheeks, Kipper and Piper came as close to being two peas in a pod as they could be without being twins. Besides, in Emily's dress pocket, at that very moment, was a crumpled bit of paper that smelled beautifully of fish! If Piper had but known it, there was hardly a need for him to apologize for the condition of that bit of paper. For to Emily, it was the most wonderful reminder of the fishy smell that accompanied Kipper whenever he arrived from his pa's shop. And at that moment, it was worth more to her than any crown jewel from anywhere in the whole world!

16

The Final Proof

It was several days before Piper returned with a fish. "Even fresher'n the last!" he informed Mrs. Slump.

Of course, this second time around, Piper needed no "credentuals," as he put it, because Mrs. Slump welcomed him with open arms. For, in truth, she not only enjoyed "goormette" cooking, but also enjoyed "goormette" eating. And considering the prodigious amount of taste testing that went on, it could be said that she particularly enjoyed her new specialty of the house, potato, turnip, and fresh fish stew. She even went so far as to give it a name, Slump's Supreme Surprise!

Mrs. Spilking, for her part, as was later reported to Emily by Bella, appeared ready to call out "a flippin' brass band" when informed that Piper had returned with yet another fish. It was "a crying shame," said Bella, that "that penny-pinching old witch" was getting an all-but-free fish because of Piper needing to "bribe" his way in to see Emily.

Bella, needless to say, as well as Lucy and Sarah, had all been joyfully apprised by Emily of Piper's connection to her old friend Kipper. But all three agreed with her that his report from Kipper regarding Sugar Hill Hall probably had nothing whatsoever to do with the fate that had befallen her. Perhaps another letter from the same source would simply announce that furnishings, lights, and people had returned to Sugar Hill Hall, so there would be no mystery left to connect to Emily.

In any event, when Piper returned, he had no report to bring of another letter from his uncle Ab. When Emily hurried into the kitchen, however, having been advised of his presence by a nudge and a wink from Bella, he was thoughtful and far less bright and cheery than he had been on his first visit. It was as if he *did* have something important to relate, and was just trying to make conversation until he got around to it.

At last, looking up from a not-too-successful

attempt at cleaning fish scales from the sink, he hesitated and then blurted out, "Emily, don't know as how I should be saying anything 'bout this, but Pa was telling me 'bout a man what come into his shop th'other day. Pa figgered he was a dockworker from the way he was dressed. Pa ought to know. His shop being down by the wharves, dockworkers come in all the time. This one had his wife with him, and begging your pardon, Emily, Pa said as how she looked like she was just 'bout getting ready to increase their family."

Piper's already-ruddy cheeks turned even ruddier at this. He shifted in embarrassment from one foot to the other. "Anyways," he finally continued, "this man and Pa got to talking a bit, and he tells Pa as how he's a dockworker all right, as Pa guessed, but he's been working 'board ships and just come all the way from India. He said he ain't been back long. Told Pa how glad he was to find Pa's shop, on 'count o' they live nearby."

Piper stopped to take a breath, and suddenly started staring at the toes of his shoes as if finding it difficult to look into Emily's eyes. Then at last he looked up. "Emily, . . . you don't got any reason to suppose this is your aunt and uncle, do you?"

"No, no!" exclaimed Emily. "Uncle Twice has a business in India. He's not a dockworker or even a ship's sailor. Just because the man your pa talked to has come from India doesn't mean anything. I expect there are lots of sailors on the wharves who've come from there."

Piper then turned his attention to flicking a fish scale from the sink with his fingernail. "Lots of dockworkers who are tall and handsome and got hair the color o' corn silk, like yours, Emily? And maybe a pretty little wife with dark curls as well?"

"Maybe not lots, Piper," replied Emily, finding herself becoming a trifle upset with Piper for going on with this discomforting subject. "But I'm sure there are enough."

Piper then raised his eyes, looking directly at Emily again. It appeared that he had no intention of giving up. "Dockworkers and their pretty wives who—who call each other 'William' and 'Fanny'? Ain't those names got any meaning for you, Emily?"

Emily's heart jumped to her throat. William and Fanny! Aunt and Uncle Twice! But it could not be. How could it *possibly* be? Uncle Twice was a businessman in India, not a dockworker on the wharves of New York, just as she had told Piper.

This had to be a very strange quirk of fate. It could not possibly be anything else.

"Emily," said Piper, "Pa, taking note of the condition of this man's wife, asked them if they might like me to bring a fish or two 'round to where they live, it being close by and all. Then she could choose what she likes, and ain't got to walk to Pa's shop to do it. Pa said you couldn't believe as how they thanked him for his kindness. Then he whipped out a piece o' paper so the man could write down his name and where they lived. Pa put it in a drawer and never looked at it till this morning. Then he showed it to me. We talked 'bout it, and Pa and me both decided we shouldn't do anything 'bout it till it got showed to you. So, Emily, here 'tis!"

Emily looked down at the scrap of paper handed her by Kipper and saw there, besides the address, a name in oh-so-familiar handwriting:

William Luccock

"You ain't going to faint nor anything, are you?" Piper asked anxiously. "Blood's all gone from your face, Emily."

Emily shook her head, although, in truth, she

felt almost as stunned as she had when she first saw the peppermints in the Front Room. Aunt and Uncle Twice back in New York! And while they may not have been there very long, surely it was long enough to come see *her.*

"Pa knows your story from Uncle Ab's letters, Emily," said Piper. "And I told him what you said 'bout your aunt and uncle not wishing you to live with them anymore. Pa says he don't understand it, that nice couple being so mean. But he says we ain't going to say anything to them 'bout seeing you 'less it's what you want. Pa thinks, though, it's what ought to be done."

"Oh, no! No! No!" cried Emily. "You and your pa mustn't tell them anything! They may not wish to see me. But—but perhaps they intend to come and just have not had the time."

Just have not had the time! Oh, what a very sorry excuse that would be! For if Aunt and Uncle Twice still cared deeply for Emily, would they not have rushed to see her the very moment they returned? But just to have not had the time! The words lay like stones in the room, and for several moments silenced them both.

"Please don't tell them what's happened to me

if you see them," Emily pleaded. "I—I want to wait a while longer for them to come. I'm certain they will! Promise me you won't tell them, Piper. Please promise me!"

"All right, I promise. And I'll tell Pa to promise, as well. But he ain't going to like it, Emily. I'll tell you that right now!" said Piper.

Piper left with yet a second promise that he would be back soon, no matter what. No matter what! Ominous words again. For to Emily, "no matter what" meant that Aunt and Uncle Twice might never come to see her. And if they did not come to see her, it could hardly be because they did not have the time but more likely because they did not wish to see her and then have to decide what was to be done with her. In a word, they did not wish to be bothered!

Mingled with all these thoughts that kept tumbling through Emily's head was the question, why had Uncle Twice returned with Aunt Twice from India? And why not as the businessman he had gone to India to be, but as a dockworker living near the wharves? The question kept coming back and coming back, until at last Emily came up with the answer. Uncle Twice had lost her fortune by not managing it properly. Did it not stand to reason that he might have lost his business for the very same reason? Still, whatever that reason was, and whatever the sad results, should not Uncle Twice at least have come to tell Emily how sorry he was for what had happened to her fortune? And know about it he must, for had not his friend Mr. Slyde sent him a letter asking him what was now to become of Emily?

These questions ended up in such a muddle in Emily's head that finally she could not bear to think of them anymore. At any rate, what difference did the answers make? What did she care that she was no longer an heiress or that Uncle Twice had become a dockworker? All she wanted was to be back with him and Aunt Twice and, yes, Baby Twice as well, and she might never be. Not ever again! And so for the first time since she had been sent to Mrs. Spilking's Select Academy for Young Ladies, the night following Piper's return visit, Emily cried herself to sleep.

Emily found it impossible to keep her mind on her work the following two days. Perhaps this was because she had kept her thoughts and her questions all to herself, somehow unable to reveal to Bella, Sarah, and Lucy what Piper had told her. But that night, she intended to tell Sarah and Lucy, and the following morning to tell Bella when they were doing the laundry together.

That afternoon, when the girls had left for their "exercise" period, Emily was deep in thought as she dusted the Front Room. Not paying enough attention to what she was doing, she rose too quickly from cleaning the legs of Mrs. Crumble's wing chair. Her shoulder struck the red-velvet-covered table, and at least seven peppermints parted company from the rest and plummeted to the floor. Horrified, Emily snatched them up and quickly began to set them back in the bowl, trying to remember exactly how they were placed. But she was not quick enough!

"So!" said a chilling voice from the doorway.

Emily whirled around to see Mrs. Spilking standing there with her arms folded and her eyes flaring.

"Some people never learn lessons!" she snapped. "And what do you have to say for yourself, Emily Luccock, for this act of disobedience? You know the peppermints rule, I believe? Will you please explain yourself?"

Explain the peppermints, when she stood there holding the evidence in her hand? Why, there was no excuse or explanation in the world that would do the slightest good, unless it was perhaps accompanied by dropping dead at Mrs. Spilking's feet, and there were even grave doubts about that.

Emily simply stood there barely able to breathe, much less provide an explanation.

"I thought you could not possibly have anything to say for yourself," said Mrs. Spilking with relish. Then she offered up a sigh no doubt manufactured for the occasion. "Well, you already know the punishment for this particular crime, so at least I need waste no time in describing it to you. However, in this instance, you will not only be spending one night in the Cupboard, but perhaps several nights while I make arrangements for you to occupy another of the cellar rooms. For as it appears that the kindness and warmth of my heart have not influenced you in the least, we shall no longer be awaiting word from your uncle, nor the arrival of a new student to take your place in your present room.

"You, Emily Luccock, will now be assigned to the servants' quarters in the cellar, where you should have been put in the first place. I shall personally see that your clothing is removed to the cellar before escorting you to the Cupboard tonight. And, as you are not to be trusted, you will now in my presence please replace the peppermints stolen from the bowl!"

Silently, Emily did.

Spending the night in the cellar, needless to say, no longer frightened Emily at all. She was in the cellar so much now, fetching and carrying, she was quite used to it. Then, too, she would be seeing Wolf—no, Willa—again. What if Mrs. Spilking knew about *that*! But Emily desperately did not want to spend the rest of her life in a cellar. And now that Aunt and Uncle Twice had not even come to inquire about her welfare, was that not final proof of their intentions? More and more, it looked as if life in a cellar was what was in store for her.

That night, this one grim thought chained itself inside her head and would not let go. The rest of her life to be spent living in a cellar! The rest of her life! But all the while, as she lay awake on the hard cot, unable to go to sleep, she was rubbing Willa's soft ear. For, of course, as soon as Mrs. Spilking had left, Emily had crept to the door of the Cupboard and let Willa in. Then all at once, Emily remembered something Bella had said. "I feel real scared going 'bout nights most times, but never when I'm with Willa."

Then Emily began thinking of the outlandish idea Mrs. Crumble had once tried to put in her head, the idea of fleeing. Well, suppose she were to flee now? She need no longer be afraid of Wolf . . . no, Willa again . . . tracking her down and ripping her to shreds. No, for she would actually take Willa with her, to protect her! But if that were to be the case, it meant she would have to leave that very night. For even if she were to remain in the Cupboard for several additional nights, it would not be as a "punishment," so "Wolf" would not be posted outside to guard the room.

Fleeing! Emily's heart began to race. Fleeing! But to where? She had but one place, Coddy's Fish Shop that belonged to Piper's pa. She had the address right on that fishy bit of paper she had kept in her dress pocket. But what after that? She could hardly just appear on their doorstep and expect to live there indefinitely. No, but Uncle Twice had given Piper's pa his and Aunt Twice's address. She could appear on *their* doorstep and plead with them not to send her back to Mrs. Spilking's Select Academy. Surely they would not send her back to be a servant there and live once more in the cellar, as she had in Sugar Hill Hall. They *could* not! They would have to think of something else to do with her.

Was the thought of fleeing rash, reckless, and stupid? Lucy and Sarah would think so, and they would be right. Yet even as Emily was thinking that "smart" should win out over "brave" and that she should remain right where she was, she knew "brave" was nudging "smart" right out of the way.

"And you'll come with me, Willa," she whispered in the dog's ear as she climbed from the cot. "Yes, you will!"

The part of the cellar that held the Cupboard was in total darkness, but Emily had been down there enough now to know how to make it to the door leading to the street, exactly where the trunk room was, and where in that room she had seen a rope that would serve as a leash for Willa. As for the coat and bonnet Emily would need, they were in the heap outside the Cupboard with her other clothes, spitefully thrown there by Mrs. Spilking.

The first thing Emily did was put on her coat and bonnet. Then she felt her way to the trunk room, with Willa docilely following right beside her. She found the rope easily and tied it to Willa's collar. The big dog's tail started wagging furiously, for she recognized what this meant.

The last thing Emily did was look for her trunk. This proved more difficult than she had thought, but when she finally found the trunk she believed to be hers, she opened the lid and felt the lining. And they were still there, the two gold coins! Quickly she tore open the stitching and pulled out the coins, dropping them into her coat pocket. Now she was ready!

By the time she and Willa reached the door to the street, her heart was pounding so hard she was finding it difficult to breathe. It would have been much easier to simply turn around and head back to the Cupboard. But she unlocked the door and opened it without even hesitating, for she knew if she hesitated for even a moment, she and Willa would indeed be heading back.

With the door closed behind them, she leaned down and whispered into the dog's ear, "Come along, Willa. We're going for a nice long walk!"

17

Something Fishy

Emily had been out late at night but once in her life. That had been when she was escaping from the Remembrance Room in Sugar Hill Hall to Kipper's pa's fish shop. Now she was escaping from the Cupboard in Mrs. Spilking's Select Academy to Piper's pa's fish shop. But whereas she had Kipper by her side on that earlier occasion, she did not have Piper by her side now as she hurried up one street and down another, most deadly dark but for the occasional tiny pool of light fluttering timidly around each post holding a gas lamp. Now all Emily had with her was Willa. So when a hulking shadow emerged from a black stairwell, she was nearly paralyzed with fright as the shadow drew closer and became a man. But met by a deep, throaty growl, he all but ran past them. Oh, yes,

Bella was indeed right about having Willa by one's side at night!

Emily was worried, though, that Willa might present a problem. Remembering how very long the ride was when Mr. Crawstone brought her to Mrs. Spilking's Select Academy from the wharves, not to mention Piper saying he had had to take a "bunch o' trolleys" to get there, Emily knew she could not walk to Coddy's Fish Shop or find her way there by trolley, assuming she would be allowed on one with a large dog in tow. So she must take a cab to her destination, but what cab-driver would accept a large dog as a passenger any more than a trolley? Well, she must find any cab at all, and that meant seeking a busy street.

As very large cities have countless streets that remain awake all night, Emily soon found one, but it proved to be more frightening than streets that were dark and deserted. Cruel faces with shifty eyes, painted faces with glittering eyes, and flat faces with no expression at all in their eyes all swirled around her. There was not much doubt that the gold coins in a young girl's pocket, at least one of which must be used to pay her cab fare, would not have remained in her pocket long but for the large black dog attached to a rope wrapped firmly around her hand. As it was, everyone coming in her direction carefully described a wide circle around her on the sidewalk, especially when Willa delivered her deep, warning growl.

Emily was quite right, however, in thinking no cab would take her and a big dog. They all turned her down. But in the end, she came upon one cab-driver who was actually nodding in his seat for lack of business. Emily reached up and tapped his shoe. She had to tap again before he came to with a start.

"I—I'd like to hire your cab?" she said, her voice quavering.

"You and your pet both, I presumes?" said the cabdriver. "Does he bite?"

"He's never bitten *me*," Emily replied firmly, though her knees were shaking.

"You got the money to pay?" the cabdriver asked suspiciously.

"I—I have a—a gold coin," said Emily, reaching in her pocket to draw it out and show it to him.

"Never mind," the cabdriver said quickly. "You don't better go pulling anything like that out for this lot 'round here to see, dog or no dog."

"I need to go to the wharves," said Emily. "Do you know where they are?"

"Do I know where the wharves is?" The cabdriver looked at her in disbelief. "This is New York, young lady. Just tell me where on the wharves."

"It's Coddy's Fish Shop," Emily said, and gave him the address.

"All right, you and your pet hop on in, and be quick about it," said the cabdriver. "I ain't got all night!"

The ride to the wharves was as long as Emily remembered it. In truth, even longer—or at least it seemed so, because it was getting later and later, and Piper and his pa would most certainly have long since closed up the shop and gone to bed. But at last the cab pulled to a stop, and Emily climbed out with Willa.

When she handed the cabdriver a gold coin, however, his eyebrows raised almost to his hairline, and he whistled. "Wheeoo! So you really do got a gold coin. But I got to tell you, I don't got change for a king's ransom. Maybe somebody here can help out, but looks like the place is closed down for the night."

Coddy's Fish Shop was indeed closed, and it was

dark upstairs as well as down. And if there was any doubt about the matter, a streetlight lit up a sign on the door that unmistakably read CLOSED!

The cabdriver frowned. "Young girl like you oughtn't to be traveling 'round this hour. You certain somebody's expecting you here?"

"In—in a way," replied Emily, which was a half-truth after all. For had Piper not given her this address with the idea that some day she might need it? And was this not that some day?

"You best make certain, miss," replied the cabdriver, leaping down beside Emily. "I'll come with you while you go knock."

So it was the cabdriver and Willa who accompanied Emily to the door of Coddy's Fish Shop, where she timidly knocked. Then, noting a small brass button beside the door, she hesitated but then pushed it.

Somewhere in the shop a bell rang. Several anxious minutes passed before Emily saw through the glass in the door a light descending a stairwell at the back of the store. It was followed by a man and a boy, both in their nightclothes. Yawning, they came to the door, and the man unlocked and cautiously opened it. If the man was not Piper's pa, it must be said that considering his red hair, blue eyes, and ruddy cheeks, he was certainly a fine imitation of that person.

"Shop's closed," he said, scowling. "Can't you see the sign?"

At this point, Piper, for it was indeed he, gave his pa a sharp dig in the ribs. "This here's Emily, Pa," he said, and then produced a sunny grin bright as the middle of day. "Evening, Emily!"

"Emily? Well, I never!" exclaimed Mr. Coddy, his expression changing from the very cold north one hundred eighty degrees to the warmest south imaginable. "But, child, what are you doing out at this time of night?"

"Same as I was wondering, sir," said the cabdriver. "I being the one what brung her and her dog here. But if it ain't too much trouble, she give me a gold coin I ain't got any way in this world o' changing. Might I be asking if you got any way o' changing it for her, and helping me out? Much obliged if you could."

"I could, indeed!" said Mr. Coddy. "You are an honest man not to be taking a child's gold coin and driving off with it. Now, if you can just tell me the fare for her ride here?"

In no time at all, Mr. Coddy had turned over to the cabdriver not only the fare and a generous number of extra coins, but a large fresh mackerel as well! Then, with a promise to return to Coddy's Fish Shop at the earliest possible moment as a customer, the cabdriver climbed back onto his cab and, with a smile and a tip of his cap, drove off whistling.

"I—I'm very sorry to have put you to so much trouble, Mr. Coddy," said Emily. "And it's—it's so very late at night."

"No trouble at all, child," said Mr. Coddy. "And it ain't all that late. Piper and I only just climbed into bed, being late cleaning up and closing the shop. On top o' that, you got a invitation to come here with no date nor time on it, far as I can recollect. So now's as good a time as any. Ain't that right, Piper?"

"Right, Pa!" agreed Piper, nodding his head so hard his red curls bobbed on his forehead.

"But I must pay you for my cab ride," said Emily.

"Oh, we'll have to see 'bout that!" said Mr. Coddy, with a broad wink at Piper saying clear as any words that the subject was not to be mentioned again.

"But what you need to tell us is who your friend is," Mr. Coddy then said, leaning over to rub Willa's ear. That ear and the other, of course, had already been getting a good deal of attention from Piper, and Willa's tail was flagging the air at a great rate.

"Piper never did get 'round to making mention o' any dog," said Mr. Coddy.

"That's because I never got around to telling him about her," said Emily. "Her name's Willa, but I only learned that a while ago. Mrs. Spilking, who owns the school, always tells everyone she's a boy dog named Wolf, who will rip us to shreds any chance he gets. She posts Wolf—only it's really Willa—outside the Cupboard, which is where you get put to be punished. It's where I was when I ran away here tonight, and . . . oh, it's so complicated, and it's such a long story!"

"Which you shall tell us now!" declared Mr. Coddy.

"To-Tonight?" stammered Emily.

"Why not?" said Mr. Coddy cheerfully. "We're all properly awake now. But I think it best be told up in our quarters over the shop, if it pleases you."

"Should I bring Willa?" asked Emily.

"Piper wouldn't like it if you didn't!" replied Mr. Coddy, his eyes twinkling, as he started for the stairs.

So Piper, Emily, and Willa followed Mr. Coddy up the narrow stairs, leaving behind the neat and tidy little shop that smelled of fish, and arriving at the neat and tidy little apartment above it, where the smell of fish was almost equal to that of the shop below. Emily was enchanted, for it was just as if she had been transported right to Kipper's pa's place!

They had no sooner arrived upstairs than Mr. Coddy turned to Emily and asked, "What is it you call Kipper's pa, who is also my brother Abner and Piper's uncle? You call him 'Mr. Coddy,' as well?"

"Oh, no!" said Emily. "He said he'd be pleased if I was to call him 'Pa,' which I always did."

"Well, then," said Mr. Coddy, "I'd be pleased as the crab what crawled out o' the crab pot if you called *me* 'Pa,' same as my brother Ab. Ain't any reason as I can see why you can't have two pa's. Any reason as you can see, child?"

"Oh, none at all!" replied the delighted Emily.

"Then that's settled," said Mr. Coddy, now to be known as Pa. "Piper, I'd take it kindly if you'd heat up some o' that milk we just got in fresh this morning. Then pour Emily here a cup. One o' our old saucepots will do fine for holding some water for Willa."

Those things speedily accomplished, Pa, Piper, and Emily sat down around the small table with the blue checkered cloth over it that served as Piper and Pa's dining table.

"Now," said Pa, "you're to tell us everything, starting way back with that place you call Sugar Hill Hall. Piper's told you we already been told a lot by his Uncle Ab, writing for Kipper, so it ain't all new to us."

So Emily began her story, going back to the very beginning, from when she first arrived at Sugar Hill Hall after her mama and papa had been lost in the boating accident, and she was an orphan come to live with her Aunt and Uncle Twice. She was only interrupted a very few times when Pa mentioned that, well, he already recollected being told that by his brother Ab or when he had a question about something. But there were no interruptions when she came to the part in her story where Uncle Twice had sold Sugar Hill Hall, and she had been left at the terrible Mrs. Spilking's

Select Academy for Young Ladies as Aunt and Uncle Twice departed for India. Again and again, as the sad story unfolded, Pa would shake his head, especially at the end of her tale, when Emily related how she had been condemned to the Cupboard for having stolen peppermints that, in reality, she was trying to put back in the bowl.

Pa exploded at that. "Blamed peppermints! We heard o' them wicked Sugar Hill Hall things from Kipper, writing through Abner. But where I got to come in here is to say what I told Piper, that something ain't right 'bout you thinking the nice couple I met, what turns out to be your Aunt and Uncle Twice, not wanting you 'round anymore. Can't help it, but I smell something fishy going on what ain't what's coming from down below. Just can't put a finger on it."

"But I still think I should have waited to see if they'd come to see me," declared Emily.

"I don't b'lieve so," Pa said. "I think that old witch done you a favor, if you'd like to know. Helped you find the courage to come here, just as you should. But we'll know it all tomorrow when we go to your aunt and uncle's place, which you allow as how you now wish to do. And it'll turn out just what I'm thinking. You wait and see!"

How Emily would have loved to believe what Pa said as she lay in a cot later in the cozy room that served as parlor, dining room, kitchen, and Piper's bedroom, while Piper bunked that night in Pa's tiny room. How she would have loved to fall asleep thinking only of that lovely fishiness that filled the room, reminding her so much of an earlier, happier time. As it was, all she could think of was "we'll know it all tomorrow." Tomorrow! Never had that word filled her with so much dread.

18

Something Even Fishier

It was decided that they had better wait until late in the day when Uncle Twice should have returned from his work on the docks, before Pa and Piper walked Emily and Willa to the address given by Uncle Twice. Pa thought it would not be wise to surprise Aunt Twice when she was alone, her condition being what it was. Whether it would be a pleasant or an unpleasant surprise remained to be seen, but in either case, Emily's sudden appearance might be a shock. So it was late afternoon before they set out, going on foot because, as Uncle Twice had said, they did not live far from Coddy's Fish Shop.

Although Pa and Piper attempted to carry on a cheery conversation the whole way, they failed miserably, and were largely silent when they arrived at their destination. Emily was finding it difficult to breathe as Pa lifted a hand to knock on the door. It was Uncle Twice who answered the knock, and, of course, the first person he saw standing before him was Pa.

"Don't know if you remember me, Mr. Luccock," he said. "But I'm Caleb Coddy of Coddy's Fish Shop, where you stopped by the other day. Said I'd send my boy 'round with nice fresh fish for Mrs. Luccock to choose from."

"Of course I remember, Mr. Coddy," said Uncle Twice at once. "But I never expected you to be so kind as to take the trouble to come yourself."

"Well," said Pa, "I came on account o' I got something real important to deliver, something what ain't fish!" With that, he stepped aside to reveal Emily standing directly behind him.

Before she even had time to think what was happening, she felt two powerful arms wrapped around her, lifting her off the ground and hugging her so tightly she could not even breathe.

And then Emily knew! She knew even before a word was spoken! The horror was over. She was home again at last!

"What is it, William? What is it?" came Aunt Twice's anxious voice from across the little room.

"It's Emily, Fanny! It's our Emily!" Uncle Twice's voice was choked with tears.

"Emily!" cried Aunt Twice. "Oh, William, you know I can hardly rise from this chair. Bring her to me! Bring her to me!"

Then Emily was carried across the room as if she weighed no more than a feather, and set down on the small settee beside Aunt Twice. Tears were already streaming down Aunt Twice's cheeks, mingling with Emily's own, as she wrapped her arms around her niece. "Our dearest Emily! Our darling child!" she said again and yet again.

Uncle Twice now turned back to Pa and Piper, still standing at the open doorway. "How? Why?" he asked, throwing out his hands in a gesture of helplessness. "But I beg your pardon for leaving you standing at the door. Please do come in!"

"Gladly, Mr. Luccock, but my son Piper and me got a big dog here with us what belongs to your Emily," Pa said. "Gentle as a kitten, but we don't rightly know what we should do 'bout her."

Still wiping away tears, Uncle Twice could not help laughing. "Bring her in then, man," he said. "The room is small, but I'm sure we can squeeze in a dog."

As Pa, Piper, and Willa entered the room, Uncle Twice said, "You've met my wife, Mr. Coddy, but let me introduce our visitor, Captain Seaforth. Captain, allow me to introduce Mr. Coddy, who is the owner of a very excellent fish shop nearby, and his son, Piper."

So overcome by all else happening, Emily had not even noticed the man in the captain's uniform, nearly as tall and strapping as Uncle Twice, although with steel gray hair, who had been standing quietly in a corner of the room. Now he came forward with outstretched hand to shake the hands of Mr. Coddy and Piper.

"Perhaps, William and Fanny," he said, "with you having so much to talk over with Mr. Coddy, I should put off my visit until another evening."

"No reason at all for you not to stay, Captain," said Uncle Twice.

"None whatsoever, Samuel," echoed Aunt Twice. "Please do stay!"

"Besides," said Uncle Twice, "as I'm to be working for you, nothing says you should be kept from knowing all that goes on with us. I'm afraid Piper will have to share a place on the floor with Willa, but there's a chair for you, Mr. Coddy. We anxiously await the answers to my questions as to why and how this all came about, that you should suddenly appear on our doorstep with the most wonderful gift imaginable."

However, before Pa could begin to answer the questions, Uncle Twice first needed to go over to Emily and provide her with another hug. This was followed by a hug from Aunt Twice, and then yet another from Uncle Twice. So several minutes passed before the excitement, if not the joy, had subsided. But at last, Pa, now seated comfortably in the proffered chair, could begin his story.

"Well," he said, "it all come about on account o' you handing me your name and address for Piper here to be bringing fish 'round. Happened so I never looked at it for two days, but when I did, you could o' flapped me with a flounder if it weren't a name I knowed well . . . William Luccock. You see, happens you met up with someone name o' Abner Coddy, who has a fish shop and son name o' Kipper, way th' other side o' this continent. And happens Abner is my brother Ab!"

"You don't say!" exclaimed Uncle Twice in astonishment.

"Do, indeed!" said Pa, going on to tell how even

before Aunt and Uncle Twice had appeared in Coddy's Fish Shop, he had had a letter from his brother Ab passing on news from Kipper of Sugar Hill Hall being dead empty with no one living in it. What with Kipper thinking this mighty strange, and thinking his friend Emily might like to know about it, Pa said, he nosed around until he found her whereabouts. Then away went Piper offering fish for sale cheap so he could get in to see her and pass on Kipper's news.

"After that, along comes your name put right into my hand!" said Pa. "I was in a puzzlement thinking what to do, what with the child telling Piper her aunt and uncle were off to India and didn't want her living with them anymore. Anyways, I sent Piper back to her with the news that you were here, being certain there were some mistake made. And I was likewise certain you ought to be told as how she got made a servant at that school, and—"

"Whoa! Whoa, Mr. Coddy!" Uncle Twice interrupted, throwing his hands in the air. "Emily believing her aunt and uncle don't want her living with them anymore is indeed the biggest mistake in the world, and we will absolutely prove it to her. You were entirely right in thinking what you did. But what's this about Emily being made a servant at the school? Could it possibly be true? Or could it possibly be that the school provides a course in home management for genteel young ladies, and this might be taken as being a servant, quite in error? Emily, is that it?"

At this, the already-tearful Emily burst into sobs and threw herself on Aunt Twice's shoulder. "No! No! I was made a servant, just as I was at Sugar Hill Hall. Oh, Aunt Twice, I was! I *was*! And Mrs. Spilking's Select Academy is a terrible place where we were fed the most dreadful food day in and day out because she is a pinchpenny, just like Mrs. Meeching was. And we never had any proper studies at all, so I could just as well have gone to India or any other place. All we did all day was sew and read over and over again dull books so old the covers were falling off.

"For exercise, we just walked 'round and 'round and 'round in the dirt in a tiny yard that I don't believe ever had anything growing in it. And we weren't allowed to whisper to one another. All we did was listen to Wolf barking. Only it turned out Wolf was poor Willa. Mrs. Spilking just called her that to scare us and make us believe Wolf, who was not Wolf at all, would rip us to shreds if we did things she didn't like."

This all came tumbling out and ended with Emily sobbing uncontrollably in Aunt Twice's arms.

"I don't understand," said Uncle Twice, looking bewildered. "Emily darling, why did you write to tell us how much you loved the school and how happy you were to be there? Besides the one from Josiah Slyde welcoming us and wishing me well in the new business, we received two positively glowing letters from you before we left India."

"I *had* to write them!" Emily explained, sobbing. "Everything we wrote was read by Mrs. Spilking, checking for spelling and grammar, she said. Then she mailed our letters herself. But everyone knew that if you said one bad thing about the school, the letter would never be mailed."

"Oh, William!" said Aunt Twice in dismay. "How could we have let this happen?"

Uncle Twice shook his head. "How were we to know it was such a place? Josiah told us a member of a royal family actually attended Mrs. Spilking's Select Academy, which is what persuaded us of its excellence. Was there no such person there, Emily?"

"No!" said Emily, with a long, miserable sniff.

"There's only Princess Delilla, except she isn't a princess at all. I learned of it by accident when I overheard her and Mrs. Spilking having an argument. She was calling Mrs. Spilking 'Ma,' and Mrs. Spilking was calling her 'Dolly.' Bella, who is the maid there and is my friend, found out about it as well. Princess Delilla is really only Dolly Spilking, Mrs. Spilking's daughter! And she got me in dreadful trouble, making me go on an errand for her that I shouldn't have, and I got put in the Cupboard for punishment."

"The Cupboard? What is that, Emily dearest?" Aunt Twice asked. "It sounds dreadful."

"It is, Aunt Twice!" cried Emily. "It's like the Remembrance Room in Sugar Hill Hall, only Wolf was stationed outside the door to rip me to shreds if I tried to escape. But that's when I learned Wolf, who is really Willa, would no more have done such a thing than Clarabelle, the kitten!"

"Threatening young girls with being ripped to shreds!" exclaimed Aunt Twice. "Oh, William, how could Josiah have been so misled in recommending this horror of a place? And to think we left Emily in that—that woman's hands!"

"Well," said Uncle Twice, "he must have been

misled in turn by his friend Mr. Crawstone, who'd heard the school praised by so many of *his* friends. Perhaps they've all been misled."

Emily hesitated. "I—I believe Mr. Crawstone just told Mr. Slyde about the school because he's good friends with Mrs. Spilking himself. I had to sit outside the door of Mrs. Spilking's parlor the night Mr. Crawstone took me to the school. She was serving him tea and calling him 'Ichabod,' and he was calling her 'Sophronia.'"

Upon hearing this, Captain Seaforth broke in. "You know," he said thoughtfully, "I pray you don't mind my offering an opinion, but I believe your niece may be right. New York is a big city, and there could be another with the name of Ichabod Crawstone, but I strongly doubt it. And if he's the man I believe he is, I've heard of him, a lawyer with a very unsavory reputation. I wouldn't be surprised to know that he's steering students into Mrs. Spilking's Academy on his own and concocting that tale about a resident princess."

"Then we've all been badly misled," said Uncle Twice, "and at our darling niece's expense! What a terrible, terrible thing we have done to her. But, Emily, with all of this, you have yet to explain what you meant in saying you are now a servant at the school. What did you mean by that?"

"Uncle Twice," said Emily, "didn't you get the letter your friend Mr. Slyde wrote telling that all the money that was my fortune was lost, and asking what was to be done with me? Mrs. Spilking had me read the letter he wrote to her about it. He said he knew her academy wasn't a charity school, and he threw me upon her mercy. So she made me a servant. That's when I accidentally spilled the peppermints, and she found me when I was putting them back. So I was sentenced to the Cupboard again, only then she said I must live in the cellar ever afterward. So last night I ran away and came to Mr. Coddy and Piper."

"Peppermints again!" said Aunt Twice in despair, for she, too, knew of the peppermints always kept as a temptation in Sugar Hill Hall. "Is it a universally accepted idea that anything so delightful should be misused in such a dreadful way?"

Needless to say, no one present even attempted to answer that question.

"But did I hear you correctly, Emily?" Uncle Twice asked. "Did you say Mr. Slyde wrote that your fortune was lost?"

Emily nodded.

Uncle Twice then threw his face in his hands. "Yet another terrible blunder. Three in all . . . India, our precious niece left in the hands of that monstrous woman, and now this, losing her fortune. And all due to me!"

"Come now, William," said Captain Seaforth. "When we were fortunate enough to have met when you were working on one of my ships, I was convinced that you were many cuts above the average dockworker, with your intelligence and knowledge of seafaring. And recognizing you for the gentleman you are, I never hesitated in asking you to come and work for me in the management of my shipping company. I've had no reason to regret my decision, nor do I now. When you confided in me the so-called mistakes you've made, I believed you to be a victim of some very unfortunate circumstances, and I continue to believe it."

"But losing my beloved niece's fortune entrusted to me by my brother in his will! How could I have made such bad judgments as to lose it all?" said Uncle Twice. "But why have I never heard of this from Josiah himself? Well, I suppose considering the length of time it takes to reach India, the letter may still be on its way there, on its way back, or even lost."

"But, Uncle Twice, why didn't you and Aunt Twice come to see me at once when you returned, even if you *did* think I was happy at Mrs. Spilking's Select Academy?" asked Emily tearfully.

"Because, my sweet Emily," replied Uncle Twice, "it was exactly because we thought you were so happy that we didn't come to see you. We didn't want to distress you with how badly things had turned out for us. But we were going to come to you as soon as I started working for Captain Seaforth, and we could promise a better life for you. In only a day or so, we would have written Mrs. Spilking, informing her that we would be coming to see you."

"But why did things turn out badly for you and Aunt Twice?" Emily asked. "Did—did your business fail?"

Uncle Twice shook his head. "There *was* no business, Emily," he said sadly. And then he went on to relate the grim tale of what had befallen them in India.

They had arrived after a treacherous sea journey to find that the owners of the business purportedly purchased by Uncle Twice knew nothing of any sale. They had, in truth, never had any intentions of selling it. Further, they did not even know why letters addressed to Uncle and Aunt Twice had been sent to them. They only kept the letters in case someone named William Luccock should appear. That, of course, is how they received the letters from Emily and Josiah Slyde.

Fortunately, Uncle Twice had enough money to provide for lodgings for himself and Aunt Twice. With his seagoing experience, and asking for no pay but a berth for Aunt Twice, he was able to hire on to a ship in ten days. During that time, Emily's second letter came.

As soon as they returned to New York, Uncle Twice wrote Josiah Slyde, and had received a reply. It appears that he had had no doubts that the documents making Uncle Twice owner of the business were genuine. But he must have been duped, he said, and would do everything in his power to rectify the situation and see that Uncle Twice's losses were made up to him.

After Uncle Twice had finished telling this terrible tale, a long and deep silence fell over the small room. Then, at last, Pa spoke.

"Begging your pardon, Mr. Luccock," he said, "but in the letter you got *here,* which must o' been writ after Emily got word from the same party that her fortune were gone, shouldn't he o' said something on that matter to *you*?"

Uncle Twice looked startled. "I believe you're quite right, Mr. Coddy. No apologies necessary. He most certainly should have said something, at least mentioning a letter he sent me to that effect that went to India."

"What exactly *did* he say, William?" asked Captain Seaforth. "I mean to say, beyond speaking of the business?"

"Why," replied Uncle Twice, "he simply said that Mrs. Spilking had written him when he made Emily's tuition payment, telling him how well she was doing and how happy she was. He assured me that he was taking care to see that payments to the school were made promptly, and I had nothing to worry about on that score."

"Begging your pardon again," said Pa. "But when Emily said as how she believed she wasn't wanted on account o' you not coming to see her, I said something 'bout that sounding mighty fishy to me. Well, all this 'bout what your friend is or ain't writing you sounds fishier'n that. And I ain't talking fresh fish, neither!"

"Mr. Coddy," said Captain Seaforth, "I agree with you wholeheartedly. 'Fishy' is definitely the word for it! And I tell you what I'd like to do, William, if it's all right with you. I'm certain my attorney has connections out on the West Coast who can find out something about your Mr. Slyde. I realize you consider him a friend, but it sounds to me as if you haven't known him very long, and it can't hurt to look into it quietly. What law firm might he be with?"

"Screwitch, Chizzle, and Slyde," replied Uncle Twice. "And it's certainly all right with me, as long as it's done discreetly. If he turns out to be what I've believed, and this is all some misunderstanding, I wouldn't want him thinking I'd been investigating him."

"You may trust me on that score, William," said Captain Seaforth. "If nothing else is accomplished, I'd like to see Mrs. Spilking's Academy put out of business. Why, if I thought for one moment that my granddaughter Lucy were in a place like that, I'd be down there this minute tearing the place apart with my bare hands. Then I might do the same to my son-in-law Marcus Goodbody for putting her there!"

"B–B–But one of my roommates was Lucy

Goodbody," stammered Emily. "And—and she did say she had a grandpapa who'd been at sea since her mama died. She said one day she intended to run away and go to him, if she could find him."

At this, Captain Seaforth jumped to his feet. "Lucy Goodbody? Are you certain, child?"

"Oh, yes!" declared Emily. "She has the prettiest red curls, and—"

"By all that's holy!" said Captain Seaforth furiously. "That is indeed my granddaughter. But what is she doing in a place like that? Did she ever tell you, child, how she came to be there?"

Emily, overwhelmed with all that had transpired, had to take a few moments to collect herself. She knew that Captain Seaforth was very angry, but she knew he would want the truth, and that is what she intended to tell him.

So she related how all the girls at Mrs. Spilking's Academy truly believed they were sent there because they were not wanted at home. That is why, said Emily, it was easy for her to believe that she was no longer wanted by Aunt and Uncle Twice.

But Sarah, her other roommate, Emily said, had a pretty stepmama who considered Sarah so plain, she could not bear to have anyone think she was Sarah's mama. When she learned she was to present Sarah's papa with a new addition to the family, she easily persuaded him to send Sarah off to boarding school.

Lucy's stepmama, continued Emily, was not only pretty but also very, very young. She did not wish anyone believing she had a daughter as old as Lucy. She was also to present Lucy's papa with a new addition to the family. Lucy did not think her stepmama was very happy about that, either, only she could not very well send the baby away. But Lucy could be sent to boarding school. So she was.

"This is intolerable!" exclaimed Captain Seaforth. "And I beg the pardon of all present for saying this, but my son-in-law will live to regret marrying that bubbleheaded, vain little creature. Yet I have only myself to blame for what's happened to my poor Lucy. For when my beloved daughter Lucille was no more, I found it too painful to look at Lucy, who was so much like her. So I simply went to sea and stayed there. What I did was far worse than what you did, William and Fanny, for your motives were the highest. But I won't let another moment pass without making this right. Will you all pardon me if I leave at once to take her away from that miserable place?"

Permission instantly granted by Aunt and Uncle Twice, Captain Seaforth started for the door, but then came to a sudden stop. "Stay!" he said. "My storming over there to pull Lucy away a day after Emily disappears from the school may very well raise suspicions on the part of Mrs. Spilking. I don't want to do that in case there is even the remotest chance that there is some unwholesome connection between Crawstone, Slyde, and Mrs. Spilking. Emily, I trust in your judgment. Do you truly believe Lucy is quite safe at this school?"

"Yes," Emily said. "And Lucy will never be punished as I was. She and Sarah have never done anything to earn a single demerit."

"Then we'll wait the several days until my attorney can write and get word back," said Captain Seaforth.

"Begging your pardon again," said Mr. Coddy. "But my feelings ain't been wrong 'bout some other things, and now they're telling me waiting ain't the way to go. Ain't there anybody 'round here what can be found to give you what you might be needing to know?"

"We certainly can't be talking to Mrs. Spilking, Mr. Coddy," said Uncle Twice. "Bella, the maid known to Emily, could probably be of no help. Is there no one else at the school we could get to, Emily, someone who might not be in Mrs. Spilking's control?"

Emily hesitated. "There's—there's Mrs. Crumble," she said. "She's Mrs. Spilking's sister, who is in charge of the girls when they do sewing and knitting and other things. She's not like Mrs. Spilking, though. The girls think she's nice and that she's just as afraid of Mrs. Spilking as they are. But, oh, Aunt Twice, she does remind me so of Mrs. Plumly that I've never trusted her. Not long ago, she pulled me aside and said if I ever thought of fleeing the school, I could come to her. She put a slip of paper in my coat pocket with her address on it. I just thought it was a trick, though, so Mrs. Spilking could catch and punish me. But . . . but what if it wasn't? What if she really did believe something terrible was going to happen to me, for soon after was when Mrs. Spilking made me a servant."

Captain Seaforth and Uncle Twice exchanged questioning glances, and Uncle Twice nodded.

"Emily, is it too much to hope that you might have kept that address?" Captain Seaforth asked.

Emily reached into the pocket of her coat lying

on the settee beside her. Although she did not remember ever taking the slip of paper out, she was not at all certain it was still there. But her fingers found it, crumpled down into the corner of her pocket where it had laid since Mrs. Crumble put it there. Quickly, she handed it to Captain Seaforth.

"William," he said, "I suggest we pay a visit to Mrs. Crumble. Whether the visit will bear fruit, we have no way of knowing. But something tells me that our good friend Mr. Coddy is absolutely right. We should lose no time in finding out all we can."

"Agreed!" said Uncle Twice. "And, Mr. Coddy, you may be certain we shall keep you apprised of all that happens. For now, if Mrs. Luccock and I went on thanking you forever, we could never thank you enough for what you have done for us this evening. Why, if it were not for you . . ." Quite overcome, Uncle Twice could not go on.

But Captain Seaforth was now beckoning him from the open door, and moments later they were gone. To find out what? It could be the answer to everything. Or the hopeless answer to . . . nothing! There was little else for those of us left behind to do but wait.

19

Trapped!

It was five hours before Uncle Twice returned, and Pa and Piper had long since left for Coddy's Fish Shop. Captain Seaforth was not with Uncle Twice, who was clearly in a great state of excitement when he arrived. After very nearly being knocked over by Willa welcoming him at the front door, he found Emily and Aunt Twice on the settee, eagerly awaiting his arrival.

"I'm happy to see Willa's here," was the first thing he said. "I feared Mr. Coddy and Piper might have taken her back to the shop for the night. I'm happier knowing she's here with you, Fanny, for I'm afraid I shall have to take Emily away with me for a while."

"And I can't come with you, I suppose?" asked Aunt Twice.

"It wouldn't be wise, all things considered," replied Uncle Twice.

"Oh, William!" cried Aunt Twice, "this isn't something dangerous, is it, having to do with what you learned from Mrs. Crumble?"

"I confess to you, Fanny, it does have a great deal to do with that, but I promise you, Emily and I will be quite safe," Uncle Twice said. "You have nothing to fear!"

But it was not until they had climbed into the cab Uncle Twice had awaiting them on the street in front of the house, and he had given the cab-driver their destination, did he say anything to Emily of what lay before them.

Turning to her, he took her hand and said, "Emily, what I promised Aunt Twice is quite true. You may be frightened by what is about to transpire, but I guarantee you will come to no harm."

"But—but what about you, Uncle Twice?" asked Emily. "Might you be harmed?"

"No more than you," replied Uncle Twice. "I promised Aunt Twice that as well."

"What is to happen that might frighten me, Uncle Twice?" Emily asked, in truth, being frightened already.

"Well," said Uncle Twice, "you've heard, I'm certain, that rats often come aboard a ship when it's docked in port, haven't you?"

Emily nodded, for that was something she had often heard from Kipper. His descriptions of some had been enough to make her skin creep.

"All right, then," said Uncle Twice. "What we're about to do is trap some very large ones. But we're going to be well protected doing it. You'll see."

"Wh-Why do I have to be there?" she asked. Protected or not, she did not like this prospect at all. Kipper's descriptions of rats had been very colorful, indeed!

"It's better not to frighten you any more than you need to be, child. You'll find out everything soon. Try to be patient. And who knows, little Emily, you might even enjoy this when you look back on it!" Uncle Twice said, squeezing her hand and managing a smile. But it was a grim smile after all.

Enjoy catching very large rats? Emily could not imagine it. Was Uncle Twice joking to make her feel better? But he would say no more about it, so Emily had no choice but to be patient and try to dispel the knot that had developed in the middle of her stomach. For despite all of Uncle Twice's assurances, she *was* frightened. And she became more so when they arrived at the wharf where the ship on which they were to do their rat catching was docked. Awaiting them off in one dark corner of the cavernous building were Captain Seaforth and another sea captain.

"Poor mite!" Captain Seaforth said, which did not make Emily feel much improved. "It's too bad she had to be brought, but it will soon be over. William, allow me to present my very good friend Captain Dockard of the good ship *Ocean Star*. If it weren't for him, we couldn't have arranged this so easily. Daniel, this is William Luccock."

"You certainly have our gratitude, Captain," said Uncle Twice as the two men shook hands.

"Samuel Seaforth would do the same for me," replied Captain Dockard.

"Is everything ready aboard?" asked Captain Seaforth.

"All men stationed at their posts," replied Captain Dockard. "Your men, six of mine, and at least five of New York's finest!"

"And what of the rats?" asked Captain Seaforth.

"I told them they could take over the lounge,"

said Captain Dockard. "They're busy in there rais-
ing glasses to one another. You've made quite a
haul, Samuel, you and William Luccock here!"

"We hope so," said Captain Seaforth. "But if
we're all set, then let's get going!"

Emily by now understood that it was not really
rats they were after. But who? She could not even
guess. All she knew was that Uncle Twice was
holding her hand very, very tightly as they treaded
quietly up the gangplank. There were men, some
in seamen's garb, some in policemen's uniforms,
stationed at every door leading from the deck. And
as soon as Uncle Twice, Captain Seaforth, Captain
Dockard, and Emily stepped from the gangplank
onto the deck, two policemen immediately closed
in behind them, standing guard over the gangplank.

The four of them soundlessly entered through
a door. Then they went down a short passage to
another door. But before opening it, Captain
Dockard put out his hand, holding back Uncle
Twice and Emily.

"Stay behind for a moment," he said. "Allow
Captain Seaforth and me to enter first." Then he
opened the door, and the two men went through it.

Although all but hidden behind them, Emily could still see in the room beyond that six people, four women and two men, were gathered. They were all dressed in the most elegant clothes, as if they were off to dine in a fancy restaurant or attend a play at a theater. One of the six, the youngest woman, looked as if she actually *were* in a play, for she was wearing a brilliant red dress overflowing with lace and black velvet ribbons, and an outrageous scarf of pink boa feathers that reached almost to the floor.

All six in the room were in a high state of merriment, having no doubt sampled liberally of the bubbling liquid in the stemmed glasses they held. The two men were prancing about, kicking their legs up in the air, and causing even more merriment on the part of the ladies.

Upon catching sight of Captain Dockard, one of the men immediately raised his glass to him. "Here's to the good captain!" he shouted. "Let's give him three cheers!"

"Huzzah! Huzzah! Huzzah!" All six nearly rocked the ship with their cheers.

"And here's my good friend Captain Seaforth with me," said Captain Dockard jovially.

"Then three cheers for him, too!" shouted the second man.

"Huzzah! Huzzah! Huzzah!" They once again all enthusiastically obliged.

"Captain Seaforth, you will be pleased to know," said Captain Dockard, "has brought you all a very nice surprise!"

"Then let's have it!" called out the first man. "We all like surprises!"

With that, Captain Seaforth stood aside and motioned to Uncle Twice, still holding tightly to Emily's hand. As the two of them entered the room, a glass dropped to the floor, the sound of it splintering like a clap of thunder in the room that suddenly fell silent as a tomb. The faces of the six revelers went deathly white, as if all their blood had drained right out of their elegant shoes. They stood like marble statues, their eyes fixed, staring.

"Ah, I see that some of you recognize me," said Uncle Twice, calm and unruffled as a windless day at sea. "And most of you recognize my niece, Emily Luccock, whom I strongly suspect you had hoped would be lost in the big city, never to be seen or heard from again. But she happens to be a young person who was resourceful enough to survive, find us, and enlighten us on a great many things. A great many, indeed! It grieves me to have to disappoint all of you, but as you see, she is alive and well, brought here tonight so you can have no doubt of it!"

This said, Uncle Twice passed Emily's hand to Captain Seaforth, who took it and held it as tightly as Uncle Twice had. So tightly and safely, in truth, that Emily soon found herself no longer trembling.

"Now, I am sure you are all anxiously awaiting personal greetings from me," Uncle Twice continued smoothly. "So here you are, Theodosia Sly Meeching and Prunella Blossom Plumly, released from prison, it appears. How very nice to see you once more!

"And Mr. Crawstone, who so kindly transported my niece to Mrs. Spilking's splendid Select Academy for Young Ladies, as recommended to him by his many dear friends. It's a pleasure to be meeting you again, sir!

"As for you, my great good friend Josiah Slyde, what can I say to you, you who have done so much for me and my family? It is simply beyond my powers of speech to tell you how happy I am to see you again!

"And now, if you will pardon me for a moment, I must consult with my niece," Uncle Twice said, bowing to his audience of six, then leaning over and whispering something in Emily's ear. She, in turn, whispered back.

"Ah, yes," he continued, "I believe I am also now addressing the fabled Mrs. Spilking and—and the member of a royal family who graces her fine establishment, Princess Delilla."

Uncle Twice now paused, as if to give any one of the six the opportunity to say something about how pleased they were to see and meet *him*. But, in truth, they all appeared too paralyzed to say anything at all.

"Well," Uncle Twice continued, sighing deeply, "it grieves me to announce to you, my good friends, that all doors and exits from this ship are being guarded, and several members of the police force stand ready to escort you from the ship. Is there anything you now wish to say, or would you rather wait to explain yourselves from your jail cells?"

This brought one of the six to life at last. It was Mrs. Spilking. "How dare you come barging in here with this announcement?" she snapped, her eyes flaring in the usual manner. "We are all here to escort Princess Delilla back to her country. This is a gross insult, and her country will be deeply offended."

"Oh, come, Mrs. Spilking," said Uncle Twice. "This ship carries you all to a South American country that knows no royalty, to begin with. To end with, Princess Delilla is no more a princess than my niece or anyone else at your school. She is Dolly Spilking, your daughter, as my niece inadvertently discovered. Have you anything further to say to that?"

"Simply that your niece lies, Mr. Luccock," said Mrs. Spilking coldly. "She has even been punished for doing so."

"So I understand," said Uncle Twice, making no effort to hide his amusement, "with a dog posted outside her door who would rip her to shreds, I believe."

"I'm sure she deserved it!" snarled Mrs. Meeching. "She lied at Sugar Hill Hall as well, did she not, Plumly?"

"She is an accomplished liar," said Mrs. Plumly, an accomplished actress who somehow managed to have her rouged cheeks turn quite purple with outrage.

"Oh, that's right. I apologize. I forgot all about that," said Uncle Twice, further amused. For, after all, it was these two ladies who had assigned him to purgatory by accusing him of a crime they themselves had committed. Lying was a subject they were both quite familiar with, being past masters of the art!

"But none of us wishes to stand here and continue to be insulted," said Mrs. Spilking, drawing herself up in righteous indignation. "We shall gather our bags from our cabins and leave the ship. And we shall go on our own. We hardly need to be escorted."

"Oh, but we think you do," Captain Seaforth broke in. "Perhaps you didn't note that Mr. Luccock said *you* would be escorted from the ship . . . nothing about your bags. We have obtained a warrant to search your cabins, and have information that leaves no doubt as to what will be found in those bags."

"Information that you have learned from where?" inquired Mrs. Spilking, flaring her eyes directly at Emily. "From Mr. Luccock's lying niece, I presume?"

"You presume quite wrongly," said Uncle

Twice. "What we learned was from your sister, Bedelia Crumble, whom Captain Seaforth and I called upon this evening. Of course, she also happens to be cousin to Mrs. Meeching, as you are."

"That sniveling little creature," snarled Mrs. Meeching. "She was always afraid of her own shadow, and a big tattletale when we were growing up together. Might have made something of herself if she'd listened to my advice as her sister Sophronia did."

"Yes, such advice as to keeping peppermints in a bowl to entice the unwary, as you did the poor old people in your care, Mrs. Meeching!" Uncle Twice said angrily. "Heaven keep us from such wonderful advice!"

"So what exactly did Bedelia have to say to you?" asked Mrs. Spilking icily. "And how do you know *she* wasn't lying?"

"Simply because she chose to stay where she was and not be with you here tonight! That speaks as loudly and clearly as anything could," replied Uncle Twice, just as icily.

Now Mr. Slyde finally stepped forward, a broad smile on his face. "Come, come, William, I can explain everything to your satisfaction if you'll only let me. I trust you will, for our friendship's sake."

"Josiah," said Uncle Twice, "we *have* no friendship. I ask that you no longer continue to insult my intelligence by pretending that we do. As for your explanations, they are apparently not worth the paper you use to write them on. But, if you will pardon me, I now intend to tell you what will be found in your bags, and why.

"First, there will be gold and jewels worth many times the value of our old home, Sugar Hill Hall, hidden there behind the paneled walls of the former ballroom by Madams Meeching and Plumly. Jailed for blackmail, smuggling, murder, and intentions to murder my wife and niece, the ladies secured the services of one Josiah Slyde, of the firm of Screwitch, Chizzle, and Slyde, to plead their case. They soon recognized that here was someone as unscrupulous as they were, who might be persuaded to participate in a very interesting scheme devised by them. As it turned out, Mr. Slyde was easily persuaded, as they suspected he would be.

"After we left for India, Mr. Slyde was able to have the ladies proved innocent of murder by claiming the charge was based only on the words of a dying old man. He had the accusations of intentions to murder and charges of blackmail dismissed for the same reason. As for the smuggling, Meeching and Plumly claimed that it was all done without their knowledge, and Mr. Slyde managed to persuade the courts of that as well.

"In the meantime, their scheme was put in place. Knowing that I was in dire straits and needed to sell Sugar Hill Hall, and knowing what was still hidden behind the walls, they had Mr. Slyde purchase it without revealing who the purchasers were.

"Wanting to get me out of the way lest I raise any questions in the future, not to mention getting the money paid for Sugar Hill Hall, it was decided that Mr. Slyde should convince me of a wonderful opportunity to purchase a business in India. There was indeed a business there, but it was never for sale, as you knew all along, Josiah. So I'm sure you can see why your explanations now would mean nothing, because your word is worth nothing.

"It is my belief that my murder was to take place in India, as in the few days I was there, I was twice attacked on the streets. I presume if I *had* been murdered, my wife would have been left to die on her own. And, of course, as this would have all taken place in a far-off foreign country where we knew no one and no one knew us, none would have been the wiser for either of these deaths.

"To ensure that there would never be any questions raised by our niece in later years, not to mention wanting to lay your hands on her vast fortune, arrangements were made to imprison Emily in Mrs. Spilking's Select Academy until the right time should come for disposing of her as well. Being persuaded of your honesty and competence, Josiah, I entrusted the management of her fortune to you while I was overseas. That fortune was all soundly invested by me, and all sold by you. There never was any catastrophic failure of any of it. So much for your explanations!

"So, ladies and gentlemen, what we expect to find in your bags will be all the gold and jewels from the walls of Sugar Hill Hall, money that was to go toward the purchase of the company in India, and the proceeds of the investments I made representing our niece's fortune. Had all your plans worked out for my demise, I suppose you would not have had to be on this ship tonight planning an escape to South America. I must offer my sincere apologies for the inconvenience to you of my niece's courageous escape from your splendid academy, Mrs. Spilking, and for my managing so quickly to arrange for the return to this country of Mrs. Luccock and myself.

"But now, unless one of you has something to add to what I have just revealed to you, I believe it is time to have you all removed to jail, where you belong!"

Uncle Twice had no sooner finished this speech, however, than the young woman in the red dress, Princess Delilla, otherwise Dolly Spilking, threw her face into the pink boa feathers draped around her neck, and began to howl.

"Am I going to have to go to jail, too? You said you had prospects for me. Is going to jail prospects, Ma? Is that your idea of prospects? Well, it ain't mine!" she bawled, and then dropped to her knees, shrieking.

"You're sounding common, my girl," said Mrs. Spilking crossly. "Get up and stop your caterwauling. It won't do you a bit of good. You're not at the school anymore."

"But she will be, Mrs. Spilking," said Uncle

Twice. "There's no reason an innocent young woman should have to pay for her mother's crimes. Mrs. Crumble is waiting for her at the school, where she will be escorted by Captain Seaforth. Her future will be decided later."

"See what you've done for me, Ma?" her daughter pointed out, sobbing.

"Oh, do be still, Dolly!" was all Mrs. Spilking had to say to her.

Now at last, Uncle Twice reached for Emily's hand. "Come along," he said. "You've been a brave girl, Emily. Now we must hurry home to tell your Aunt Twice all!"

"All"! But for Emily, what a different meaning that word now had at last!

20

Sugar Hill Hall

"Felicity Emily Luccock!" whispered Emily, looking down at the bundle she cradled so very carefully in her arms as she sat in a rocking chair beside the fireplace in Captain Seaforth's cozy parlor.

The parlor was filled with remembrances of his years at sea. Paintings of ships hung on almost every bare space on the pine-paneled walls. A rusted anchor rescued from the sea leaned solidly in a corner. Enormous pink-lined tropical seashells stood on the mantelpiece over the great stone fireplace. There was even a brass porthole, giving anyone looking through it the feeling they should be seeing the ocean instead of Captain Seaforth's prize rose garden.

But Emily at the moment was concentrating only on the important job she was performing.

And someone kneeling beside her rocking chair was seeing to it that she did. This was Felicity's anxious nursemaid, Tilly. Yes, Tilly!

Tilly, who had come all the way across the continent because Aunt Twice said she would have no other nursemaid to help with the most important task in the whole world. Tilly, who had had to stay behind when Aunt and Uncle Twice left for India. Tilly, who had gone around with such a long face when told she could not be spared that her new employers finally gave up and agreed to let her go. Tilly, who was delirious with happiness now that she was not only back with Aunt and Uncle Twice, but with the only friend she had ever had, Emily. But it was also, unfortunately, Tilly, having had the care of a baby at her recent place of employment, who was an absolute tyrant when it came to deciding the proper care for Felicity. Why, even Aunt Twice had to bow to her authority!

But Emily and Tilly were not the only guests in Captain Seaforth's parlor. For happily assembled were also Aunt and Uncle Twice, Mr. Coddy and Piper, Mrs. Crumble, who had enlisted the aid of a friend to watch over the school for that evening, and Bella, Lucy, and Sarah, who had been invited to come live with Lucy and her grandpapa, Captain Seaforth. It perhaps might be mentioned here, as well, that Aunt Twice thought Lucy and Sarah two of the most delightful girls ever, and she won Sarah's undying devotion by remarking that she thought Sarah had the most beautiful eyes she had ever seen in her life!

By now, they had all enjoyed a delicious supper of roast chicken and baked ham, all manner of vegetables, and a very rich chocolate cake, all prepared by the excellent cook whom Captain Seaforth claimed to have "borrowed" for this event from one of his ships. But the first course for the meal was an outstanding fish chowder, brought from his shop in a great black iron pot by Mr. Coddy!

As Emily rocked Felicity, she was not only being closely watched by Tilly, but by Bella as well, seated on the floor beside them. To no one's surprise, Bella and Tilly had struck up an instant friendship, and had already made grand plans to "do the shops" together every chance they had.

Across the room, at a table that was once a ship's hatch, Lucy, Sarah, and Piper had gathered, and were enjoying a rousing game of cards. Piper, if anyone had been observing, would have been seen to be blushing furiously as his red curls were compared favorably to Lucy's and his blue eyes to Sarah's, but it might have also been observed that he was enjoying himself immensely.

Across from Emily, Tilly, and Bella sat Aunt Twice and Mrs. Crumble, between whom a friendship had been struck up to the degree that they were already addressing each other as Fanny and Bedelia. Both ladies were thoroughly enjoying a conversation in which the worthy Mrs. Crumble was shocking Aunt Twice to death with tales of the horrors of her sister's Select Academy for Young Ladies.

Directly in front of the fireplace stood the three men of the party, Captain Seaforth, Uncle Twice, and Mr. Coddy. At the moment, Uncle Twice had just turned from looking somberly in the embers snapping and crackling in the fireplace. He gave a deep sigh.

"You know," he said, "it still grieves me that Fanny and I put off for one moment going to see Emily when we first arrived."

"And if you had, William," said Captain Seaforth, "weren't you intending to send Mrs.

Spilking a note announcing your impending visit? I believe that's what I heard you say."

"Yes, I did, Captain, and we would have done just that," said Uncle Twice. "Good manners would have required it."

"Then I believe that by not going, you may have saved her life," said Captain Seaforth.

"How so?" asked Uncle Twice.

"Well, the way I see it is that if you had arrived at the school only to find Emily as a servant there, Mrs. Spilking would have had to give an explanation for it. Of course, she could have instantly turned Emily back into a student for your benefit, but how could she depend on Emily not to reveal that?

"You may well then have begun investigating the reasons for Josiah's announcement that all your investments on Emily's behalf had failed, which, as we all now know, they had not. That may have effectively ended all plans of that criminal lot escaping to South America with their ill-gained millions.

"So it stands to reason that Mrs. Spilking would have done everything in her power to keep you from meeting up with Emily at this critical time.

Would you agree with my thinking?" Captain Seaforth concluded, addressing the question to Mr. Coddy.

"I most definitely do, Cap'n!" that worthy gentleman said wholeheartedly.

"I do as well," said Uncle Twice. "And I thank you inexpressibly for pointing it all out to me, Captain. It removes a great deal of my guilt."

"And well it should!" said Captain Seaforth. "Of course, you realize I have some guilt of my own to deal with, but we'll talk of that later. What I've been wondering at the moment, William, is this. You're a wealthy man now, for you'll not only be regaining all you were paid for Sugar Hill Hall, but because it was your home, all the riches stored in its walls will be yours as well, as there are no claims on it. That being said, much as it would disappoint me to lose you, for I intend to retire soon and need someone like you to run my company, I would understand if you decided not to come aboard."

"Captain," said Uncle Twice without hesitating a moment, "I most definitely *do* want to come aboard, as you put it. I feel honored to have been asked. I intend to be at work every day, and to see to it that you never regret your decision to hire me!"

"And you don't think you'll ever want to return some day to Sugar Hill Hall, which I believe you have learned from Caleb's brother still stands empty?" asked Captain Seaforth.

"Never!" said Uncle Twice. "*Never!* If for no other reason, and there are, of course, many others, I don't care to revisit the scene of all my past mistakes!"

"I can't tell you how happy I am to hear all this, William," said Captain Seaforth. Then he added with a rueful smile, "As for mistakes, we've all made them. But as long as we learn from them, well . . . But tell me, aren't there some benefits, in the end, that have come about for you as a result of your mistakes?"

"Oh, yes!" said Uncle Twice. "I had that time aboard a ship learning about the sea when I was being blackmailed by Meeching and Plumly into believing I was a murderer. The sea experience is what led to our acquaintance and your offering me the position with your company. Then, I learned a great deal about money matters in handling Emily's inheritance from her father. He, of course, had built up his part of the inheritance we both had from our own father, while I was busy squandering mine. I believe I have done quite well for Emily, though Josiah Slyde attempted to persuade everyone otherwise. But most of all, had I not made those early mistakes, I wouldn't be standing here with all of you, my very good friends!"

"Hear! Hear!" said Captain Seaforth.

"Amen to it!" said Mr. Coddy.

"There are, sadly, two people missing who would make this party complete," Uncle Twice said. "They are Mr. Coddy's brother, Abner, and Emily's good friend Kipper. If only wishes were horses . . ."

At this, Mr. Coddy beamed. "Perhaps they may be in this case! See, it's this way. Ab and me, growing up, always figgered as how we'd some day go into the fish business together, living close to the docks like we did, and our pa being a fisherman besides. But Kipper's ma wanted to try the other ocean, so off they went, and ended up staying.

"Now with Kipper's ma long gone, Ab allows as how he'd like to come back here, to visit leastways, if not more. But my thinking is he'll be wanting to stay once he gets here so we can be Coddy and Coddy like we always planned, and o' course he'll be bringing Kipper 'long with him!"

Kipper coming! Emily, having heard bits and snatches of the men's conversation taking place in front of the fireplace, had pricked up her ears upon hearing Kipper's name mentioned. Now she let out a squeal of delight. Tilly was on her feet in an instant.

"Ain't you got no sense, shrieking like that, Emily?" she whispered crossly. "Here, you just give the little precious to me, an' you're excused from the job. I ain't never in all my borned days!"

Emily gently handed Felicity to Tilly, who then immediately usurped Emily's place in the rocker. Emily lost not a moment going up to Pa.

"Is it really true that Kipper and Pa will be coming here?" she asked. "Oh, then everything would be perfect!"

"I ain't got a doubt in the world 'bout it!" said Pa. "Only thing is, it 'pears to me there's a problem we got to consider. What with you calling Ab 'Pa' and calling *me* 'Pa' likewise, well, supposing we're in the same room, who's got to answer?"

Emily must have looked so taken aback at the

question that it brought a burst of laughter from Captain Seaforth and Uncle Twice. This, in turn, earned them all glowering looks from Tilly and her good friend Bella.

"Does Piper know about Kipper coming?" asked Emily.

"Not yet, but you got my permission to run and tell him," said Pa, winking at Captain Seaforth and Uncle Twice.

Now, Emily, in truth, had been happy to be relieved of her job in the rocker. Her arm had gone to sleep, and she was envying all the merriment taking place at the ship's hatch over the card game. She flew over there now and had the great pleasure of being the first to announce to Piper the astonishing news of Kipper's almost certain forthcoming arrival!

But as the evening wore on, with Felicity having been fed and now soundly asleep in her basket, everyone gathered around the fireplace. The conversation then turned to the matter of what was to become of Mrs. Spilking's Select Academy for Young Ladies. And this appeared to be the exact right time to announce to Mrs. Crumble what, with her permission, might happen to it.

It had been Emily's idea to start with. After she had spoken to Uncle Twice about it, and he had enthusiastically agreed that it was indeed a splendid idea, they had been in consultation with Mr. Dewright, Captain Seaforth's attorney at the firm of Thinkwell, Thinkwell, and Dewright. Mr. Dewright could see no reason why the plan could not be carried out. It had to do, of course, with the fact that Uncle Twice and Emily were now wealthy. Very wealthy. Very, *very* wealthy!

They were both so wealthy, in truth, that they could take all the money needed for the purpose Emily had suggested, and still have enough left over to last them several lifetimes. And what Emily had suggested was this, that the two buildings now occupied by Mrs. Spilking's Select Academy be sold. Emily and Uncle Twice would then add whatever money was necessary to buy a much, much larger and nicer building in a much more pleasant neighborhood. And it so happened that Captain Seaforth already knew of just such a building for sale on his very own street!

Uncle Twice had directed their cabdriver to pass by it on their way to Captain Seaforth's house that afternoon, and Emily had been so excited upon seeing it, she could hardly bear it. Besides a great double-oak front door that would open onto a portico with tall white columns, there were windows, windows, and more windows that would bring light and sunshine into every room of the magnificent redbrick house. Every window, moreover, boasted shutters painted a cheerful garden green.

As for the garden itself, Emily could hardly believe what she saw. For surrounded by beautiful wrought-iron panels joined by tall brick columns were handsome, well-tended evergreen shrubs and tall oak, maple, and pine trees. But what was even more important than this was what Captain Seaforth had told them was behind the house, although that could barely be seen as they bowled by in the cab. It was a lawn—a lawn where lawn tennis and croquet could be played by the girls, and where they could have lovely outdoor picnics. There was even a brick path circling the lawn for pleasant walks. And, of course, there were flower beds everywhere, for what would a true garden be without flowers?

Emily was naturally quite ready to burst out with all this news the moment she walked into

Captain Seaforth's house, but Uncle Twice advised that they should wait for a quiet moment. And at last that quiet moment had arrived!

Emily had agreed that Uncle Twice should be the one to present the plan. This he did as soon as there was a lull in the cheerful hum of conversation of those gathered around the fireplace. While describing the building and garden, however, he made no mention of his real purpose in doing so, and made it seem that this was a house he and Aunt Twice contemplated buying for their own home. But he finally made the suggestion in the most offhand manner that he believed this house would make a splendid school, so splendid, in truth, that he would like to invest in it. Yet he would consider doing so only if Mrs. Crumble, now acting headmistress of Mrs. Spilking's Academy, would agree to be headmistress of the new school.

At this point, Mrs. Crumble, who had been listening with only polite interest, sat looking stunned for a few moments, and then burst into tears! For a while, it seemed that she would never regain her powers of speech. But when she did, she could hardly stop talking, what with thanking both Uncle Twice and Emily over and over again. She was, of course, immediately apprised by Uncle Twice of Emily's part in the plan. Then Mrs. Crumble entered into excited conversation with Emily, Lucy, and Sarah, not only putting forth her own ideas for the school, but eagerly listening to those of the three girls as well.

To begin with, there would be proper classes with proper teachers in such things as geography and history. There would be music lessons and real painting lessons and reading from interesting books that were not old and dilapidated. There would, of course, be all the wonderful outdoor activities thought of by Emily, and then there must be lots and lots of washrooms, so lining up to use one would never be heard of again. At last came the subject of food. Was there to be a new cook?

Well, here Emily felt the need to express a firm opinion. She had grown truly fond of Mrs. Slump and believed she should stay. And, as she pointed out to Mrs. Crumble, they should remember the delicious fish stew, Slump's Supreme Surprise, prepared by her when she actually was given something better than potatoes and turnips with which to work. In a word, Mrs. Slump actually was able to provide "goormette" cooking, and Emily believed she should be given the opportunity to do so. As it turned out, Mrs. Crumble shared Emily's feelings and was easily persuaded that Mrs. Slump should remain.

Bella declared that she most certainly wished to stay as well, and so she should, declared Mrs. Crumble. She would, however, no longer be the servant of all work, or "donkey of all work" as she described herself, but would be promoted to head housekeeper with at least two maids under her. She would have a special dress and wear a belt with a grand bunch of keys dangling from it, just as Mrs. Spilking had. And she would never, ever again be residing in a cellar, but would have her own sunny room upstairs. Needless to say, upon hearing this from the very lips of the new headmistress, Bella herself burst into tears!

Then there was the matter of the former Princess Delilla, now reduced to being plain Dolly Spilking. When this subject came up, Mrs. Crumble could not help sighing deeply and shaking her head in despair. Dolly, of course, would soon be old enough to determine her own future, which might include marrying the grocer's boy. Whether this would be a greater disaster for him or for her was the only question, should this unfortunate event take place.

But she was, after all, Mrs. Crumble's niece, and so, despite all, she wanted only the best for Dolly. Now that her ma was no longer around to "spoil her to death" and there was no more of "all that princess nonsense," Mrs. Crumble would make every effort to try to persuade her to avail herself of the education now to be offered at the school. She felt she might even succeed, for when Captain Seaforth, accompanied by his young aide, took Dolly back to the school from the ship that memorable night, Dolly had remarked to her aunt Bedelia that the aide had cast an approving eye in her direction. *She* apparently had likewise cast an approving eye back at him. But Mrs. Crumble had assured her that no one but a grocer's boy would look twice at her if she did not improve her mind. Dolly did not argue the point, so Mrs. Crumble felt there might be some hope in that direction after all.

As for the other girls still at Mrs. Spilking's Select Academy, they would no doubt be quite thrilled with the new prospects. But then there were the two older girls who had been there "longer than they ought," as Bella had once said to Emily. "And such lovely girls, too," said Mrs. Crumble. "What is to become of them?"

It was at this juncture that Captain Seaforth entered the conversation. He would host some balls, he said, to which the girls would be invited. He would be a whale's tail, he said, if that didn't add some spark to their lives, especially as he would also be inviting several handsome young naval officers from his ships. Captain Seaforth, always used to doing everything with great dispatch, had managed to take care of this matter with great dispatch as well. With a very satisfied look on his face, he now sat back to listen to further matters. There turned out to be three.

One was Willa. The only problem there, of course, was that everyone wanted her. But there was no question that she should now be in a home where she could have all the freedom denied her for so long, not to mention the attention she deserved. Those requirements, all concluded, would be met in the home of Aunt and Uncle Twice and the overjoyed Emily!

The second matter to be talked over was a name

for the new school, for all agreed that Mrs. Spilking's name connected to it could not be tolerated.
Did Mrs. Crumble wish the school possibly to be
called Mrs. Crumble's Select Academy? "No
indeed," was the indignant reply to the question
when it was posed to her. They would have to
come up with something else. Other names were
suggested, including Luccock School, which
Uncle Twice, Emily, and even Aunt Twice positively opposed. What, then?

In the end, Emily timidly made a suggestion
that came to her when she had seen the entry to
the proposed school. Persuaded that her suggestion would be thoroughly rejected, if not actually
laughed at, she had not dared to mention it. But in
the end, she mumbled the words, "Sugar Hill
Hall." For a few moments, there was silence. But
then to her amazement, everyone began to clap,
and her idea was unanimously approved. And so
Sugar Hill Hall it was to be!

That decided, there was but one matter left, and
that was what Emily, Lucy, and Sarah wished to do
regarding the new school, having such unpleasant
memories of the old one. But Mrs. Crumble,
although saying again and again how grateful she

was for all that was being done for her, went on to say she could only be truly happy if the three girls were to return to the school when it became the new and wonderful Sugar Hill Hall. She intended to have day students as well as boarders, so they could even choose to be either one. And though, as she said, she hesitated to use the term, she promised them that they would indeed be "royally" welcomed!

A decision on that score, needless to say, was then easily reached. But considering all that poor Mrs. Crumble had had to suffer with Dolly and "all that princess nonsense," it was just as well that, in the course of time, it was not Princess Everbold, Princess Lionheart, and Princess Strongspirit, but just plain Emily Luccock, Lucy Goodbody, and Sarah Tibbits who happily entered the great double-oak doors of Sugar Hill Hall on the very day that it opened!

Epilogue

Kipper did, in very fact, come to stay in New York, and so was able to take part with his cousin Piper in the grand opening of Coddy & Coddy Fish Shop, begun at long last by the two bothers, Abner and Caleb Coddy. But both Piper and Kipper constantly expressed wishes to Emily that *they* could have a school as nice as Sugar Hill Hall to attend. By dint of Emily pleading and pleading, Mrs. Crumble thought about this, and thought about it some more, and then made her decision. If both boys would pay particular attention to improving their speech, she might allow them, and a few other boys, into the school as day students. And so it was that when Emily, Lucy, and Sarah finally graduated from Sugar Hill Hall, Piper and Kipper proudly graduated right along with them!

BAKER & TAYLOR